CONFESSIONS OF A

Now a Columbia Pictures
starring

Anthony Booth
Doris Hare
Bill Maynard
Sheila White
and
Robin Askwith
as
'Timothy Lea'

with Guest Stars

Peter Cleall
Carol Hawkins
Peter Jones
Bob Todd
and
David Hamilton

For Ted Seago and the Boston Boppers

Timothy Lea

Confessions of a Pop Performer

J. B. MACKIE

Futura Publications Limited

A Futura Book

First published in Great Britain in 1974
entitled CONFESSIONS FROM THE POP SCENE
by Futura Publications Limited

This edition first published 1975

ISBN 0 8600 7276 2
Printed in Great Britain by
Hazell Watson & Viney Ltd
Aylesbury, Bucks

Futura Publications Limited
49 Poland Street
London W1A 2LG

CONFESSIONS FROM THE POP SCENE

Chapter One

In which a talent spotting trip to the East End with brother-in-law, Sid, involves Timmy in an unseemly fracas and two close brushes with the opposite sex.

Chapter Two

In which an attempt is made to turn nephew, Jason Noggett, into a six-year-old Mick Jagger and Timmy shares a few idyllic moments with lonely Mrs Blenkinsop.

Chapter Three

In which Timmy meets Nutter Normanton, the man who plays the piano with his head, and Reg, Fuggy, Pete and Trembler – fellow members of Kipper, the group Sid hopes is going to make Noggo Enterprises a fortune.

Chapter Four

In which Kipper makes a memorable debut at the Rollerdrome and Timmy receives succour at the hands – and other things – of Belinda Muckredge, enthusiastic cub reporter.

Chapter Five

In which Kipper strike a hard bargain and Timmy is introduced to some of the sordid realities of the pop world – and has a nice time.

CHAPTER ONE

In which a talent spotting trip to the East End with brother-in-law, Sid, involves Timmy in an unseemly fracas and two close brushes with the opposite sex.

'Gordon Bennett!' says Dad. 'Most people can get out of the nick easier than the army. "Dishonourable Discharge." Sounds like what we used to find on the front of your pyjamas.'

'Dad, please!' I mean, that kind of remark is so uncalled for. Anyhow, I never had a pair of pyjamas when I was going steady with the five-fingered widow.

'This latest disgrace has dropped us right in it with the neighbours. I don't know where to put my face.'

'Why don't you try some of the places Sid has been suggesting all these years?' It is sad, but Dad always brings out the worst in me.

'You leave your sponging brother-in-law out of this. Just consider what you've achieved in the last five years. You've broken your mother's heart and now you've damn near done for mine. In the nick twice and God knows how many jobs you've had.'

'The first time was only reform school, Dad.'

'That's shredded in the mists of antiquity, that is. Why can't you be like your sister? A nice home, two lovely kiddies. She's done all right for herself.'

'I couldn't find the right bloke to settle down with, Dad.'

'I don't expect it's for want of trying, though. That's the one thing we haven't had from you, isn't it? I'm waiting for you to turn into a nancy boy. That'll be the final nail in my coffin.'

I've started a whip round for the hammer, Dad.'

As might be expected, Dad is not slow to take umbrage at this remark.

'That's nice, isn't it? Bleeding nice. That really puts the kibosh on it, that does. You sacrifice your whole life to your kids and what do you get? Bleeding little basket wants to see you under the sod.'

'One on top of the other, Dad.'

Dad steams out of sight and I consider what an ugly, weasel-faced old git he is. It is amazing to think that he could have produced something as overpoweringly lovely as myself. Sometimes I wonder if he actually did have a hand in it – or something more intimate. I have always found it disgusting to think of my Mum and Dad on the job but the thought of some invisible third-party – a prince or something like that – giving Mum one behind Battersea Town Hall seems much more favourite. The arse is always cleaner on the other side of the partition, if you know what I mean.

Of course, to be fair, you can understand Dad being a bit narked. When I was conned into signing on as a 'Professional' for nine years he must have thought that he could fill every inch of my bedroom with nicked stuff from the lost-property office where he works. I use the word 'work' in its loosest sense. Dad had to be carried into the nearest boozer when someone in his bus queue mentioned overtime. When Dad thought he had got rid of me he reckoned without Sid's ability to put the mockers on anything he comes into contact with. I will never forget the sight of Sid's nuclear warhead drooping towards submarine level while the colonel's lady shouted for action and all those Yanks with gaiters halfway up their legs bristled in the doorway. It is the nearest we have ever come to causing World War III. She was a funny woman, that one. Very strange. There can't be many birds who fancy a bit of in and out under the shadow of the ultimate deterrent – still, I expect you read all about it in *Confessions of a Private Soldier* so I won't go on. (Of course, if you did not read about it, there is nothing to stop you nipping round the corner and having a word with your friendly local newsagent. If you ask him nicely he might be able to find you a copy – to say nothing much about the other titles in the series. For instance, there is – 'Belt up and get on with it!' *Ed.*

All right, all right! I've got to live, haven't I. Blimey, these blokes think you can nosh carbon paper. I am not surprised that *Les Miserables* packed it in after one book.)

Anyway, getting back to the present. There I am at 16, Scraggs Lane, ancestral home of the Leas since times immemorial after an unproductive brush with H.M. Forces. It might have done Mark Phillips a bit of good but I did not as much as catch sight of a corgi's greeting card the whole time I was in the Loamshires. Ridiculous when you consider how many Walls sausages the family must have eaten over the years. And talking of food, here comes my Mum, that commodity's greatest natural enemy. The only woman to have burned water.

'Stop going on, Dad,' she says. 'Tea's on the table. I've got some nice fester cream rice for sweet.'

'You mean, Vesta Cream Rice, Mum. "Fester" means to turn rotten.'

'You want to taste it before you start telling your mother what she means,' snorts Dad. 'It doesn't take a lot of prisoners, that stuff, I can tell you.' Mum may be a diabolical cook but her heart is in the right place – and that saves an awful lot of trouble when you go for a medical checkup, I can tell you. It also means that she is always glad to see me home whatever I have done. She has even tried to spell out 'WELCOME' in the alphabet soup.

'It's funny,' she says, gazing at me over the curling beefburgers. 'You look such a wholesome boy.'

Dad snorts, 'I expect Jack the Ripper looked bleeding wholesome and all. Don't start making excuses for him, mother. He's never going to change. I've given up hope for him.'

'Have you thought about what you're going to do, now, dear?' says Mum, absentmindedly straining the cabbage on to the beefburgers – at least it takes the curl out of them.

'Sid's got an idea about going into the entertainment business. I'm having a talk with him tonight.'

'"Entertainment?" But you don't do anything.'

'You can say that again,' sneers Dad.

'I know how you got that job at the lost property office,' I say. 'Someone handed you in, did they?'

'Watch it, Smart Alec!'

'Stop it, both of you. You know I can't stand scenes. I still don't see what Timmy is going to do. Sid doesn't play anything, does he?'

'Sidney Noggett has been on the fiddle for years,' says Dad wittily. 'That's the only way you get anywhere, these days. A decent working-class man with a set of principles might as well stay at home.'

'You do stay at home most of the time, Dad.'

'It's my back, isn't it? There's no cause to mock the afflicted. If me and a few more like me didn't have our aches and pains you might be feeling the Nazi jackboot across the back of your neck.'

Dad does tend to over-dramatize a bit for a bloke who spent most of World War II fire watching. In fact I have known him turn off 'Dad's Army' because he found it too harrowing. Still, he is very sensitive on the subject and since my present standing in the family is one of grovelling I should be advised to lay off.

'Sorry, Dad.' The words are more difficult to form than the Bermondsey branch of the Ted Heath fan club.

'I should bleeding think so. Young people today don't know the meaning of the word patriotism. Look at us. Knocked out of the World Cup by a load of Polaks. The Krauts going mad in Munich. It's a bleeding national disgrace.'

'Come on, Dad. When your mate, Stanley Matthews, was playing we were beaten by the Yanks.'

Dad does not like this. 'Sir Stanley Matthews if you don't mind, Sonny Jim. That was the atmospheric conditions, wasn't it? They made them play up the side of a mountain, didn't they? Our lads weren't used to it. I don't call that football.'

'Do give over, Dad,' says Mum. 'How do you like the beefburgers?'

'I don't reckon them boiled, I can tell you that.' Dad did not see Mum straining the cabbage over them.

'Just as you like, dear. I thought it might make a change.'

Mum does not bat an eyelid. 'Eat up, Timmy. Your rice is all ready.'

Already ruined, I can see that. Once it starts making a bolt for it over the side of the saucepan you can reckon that it has given up the ghost.

'I don't know if I can manage it, Mum,' I say, patting my stomach in a way that I hope suggests satisfaction with the excellent fare that has already been provided.

'Go on. I know you can find room for it. I'll put some golden syrup on it like I used to when you were a little boy. You remember how he used to love hot, sticky things when he was a kiddy, Dad?'

'Yeah.' Dad's face adapts a thoughtful expression and I can sense his disgusting mind working on time tasteless descent into vulgarity.

'Just a little bit, Mum,' I say hurriedly, 'I think I put on some weight in the army.'

'I was thinking how thin you looked.' Mum thumps down an enormous helping of what looks like petrified frog's spawn. I do wish she would not use the spoon with which she dishes out the beefburgers. 'There you are. Rice is the stable diet of the Chinese, you know.'

'This lot looks as if it's seen the inside of a stable and all,' complains Dad. 'Gordon Bennett! How do you manage to get it like that?'

'I did what it said on the side of the tin,' says Mum, patiently reading from the label. '"Brown and crisp on the outside, moist and tender in the middle."'

Dad claps his hand to his head. 'Gawd, give me strength! That's the steak-pie tin, isn't it? Can't you even read from the right bleeding labels?'

'Oh dear. It must be my glasses,' says Mum.

'Yeah, you want to stop filling them to the brim all the time,' snaps Dad.

'It wouldn't be a surprise if I did turn to drink, the way you go on at me,' sniffs Mum. 'If the food isn't good enough for you, you'd better give me some more housekeeping money.'

'I daren't do that,' says Dad. 'All you'd do is buy bigger tins.'

'At least the print on the labels would be larger, Dad,' I say helpfully.

'Don't you turn against me, now,' sobs Mum. 'I try and do you something nice when you come home and this is all the thanks I get.'

'See what you've done now?' snarls Dad. 'You've made your mother cry. As soon as you're through the door you're spreading misery and unhappiness. If what you get here isn't good enough for you –'

His voice drones on but it is a track from an L.P. I have heard a million times and the words disappear like raindrops into snow. I am meeting Sid round at his Vauxhall pad and I am not sorry when the time comes to steal away with Dad's voice melting in my ear and a fistful of Rennies belting down to put out the fire in my belly. I am also looking forward to seeing sister Rosie again. When Sid last talked about her she had started up a couple of boutiques and was doing all right for herself. Ever since her little brush with Ricci Volare on the Isla de Amor she has been a different woman from the one that used to hover in front of Sid like the pooch on the old H.M.V. label. I feel sorry for Sid. It can't be nice for a bloke to see his wife doing something on her own – especially when she starts doing better than he is. Ever since the Cromby Hotel, Sid has been marking time if not actually going backwards while

Rosie has been coming up like super-charged yeast. How will I find the girl who was voted Clapham's 'Miss Available' in the balmy days of 1966?

The short answer is – thinner. Rosie's tits seem to have evaporated and the skin is stretched over her face like the paper on the framework of a model aeroplane. She has also done something with her eyebrows – like got rid of them – and her barnet is closer to her nut that I can ever remember it.

'Got to go out, Timmy love,' she says, kissing me on the cheek. 'Sidney will give you a drink. Must fly. See you again.'

Her voice is different, too. Not exactly posh, but sharper. It carries more muscle, somehow.

Sid looks relieved when she has pushed off. 'What's your poison?' he says.

I am a bit disappointed with the surroundings. I had been expecting signs of loot, but they don't even have a cocktail cabinet. The booze is laid out on a tray and that rests on a table which is definitely on its last legs. Peppered with worm holes and dead old-fashioned looking. Most of the stuff they have got must have come from a junk shop though the carpet is nice. Probably took up all their cash.

'I'll have a light ale, since you're asking,' I say.

Sid looks uncomfortable. 'We don't have any light ale. There might be some lager in the fridge.'

I look at the tray and he is right. It is full of bottles of gin and vodka and something called Noilly Prat. That sounds nice, doesn't it? Just the kind of thing you would like to offer your mother-in-law.

'Let's go round the boozer,' I say. 'Where's Rosie pushed off to?'

Sid is already helping himself to a large scotch. 'She's gone to look at one of her wine bars.'

'Wine bars? She given up the boutiques, has she?'

Sid took a deep swig at his drink. 'She's got these as well as the boutiques.'

'What is a wine bar, Sid?'

'It's like a boozer, but they only sell wine.'

How diabolical! My blood freezes over when I hear his words. I mean, I don't mind a spot of plonk on the Costa Del Chips, that is the place for it, isn't it? But in your own local – and pushing out the native product! It hardly bears thinking about. How could Rosie do such a thing? It must be a blooming disaster.

'Making a bleeding fortune,' says Sid.

'Yerwhat?' I say.

'I thought she was round the twist but it's amazing what people go for these days. Wine is dead smart, see? And a load of birds reckon it. You get a lot of posh bints in her places. They used to think it was all spit and sawdust down the boozer and you must be on the game if you went into one. A wine bar was different. That was refained, somehow.'

'So it's just a load of judies, is it?' I say thoughtfully.

'Used to be. Until there was this article in the paper that said just that. It went on about how a bird could drink in peace without being molested and that there were thousands of little darlings sipping their full bodied rhoja—'

'Blimey, they must have been desperate, Sid.'

'That's what everybody thought, Timmo. The day after the article appeared there were blokes fighting to get through the door. Now it's just one great knocking shop.'

'Poor Rosie. She must be heartbroken.'

'Yes, she's crying all the way to the bank. Do you want to see one?'

'Not really, Sid. I've thought about opening an account but—'

'I didn't mean a bank, you berk! I was referring to one of Rosie's wine bars. We could look in later.'

'Very nice, Sid. But we've got some business to discuss, haven't we?'

'Too true, we have. All this chat about Rosie's business.'

Success has whetted my appetite. If she can do it why not her attractive brother?

'Right,' says Sid knocking back his scotch. 'Let me reiterate. I think there are some fantastic opportunities in the entertainment field. I don't mean performing ourselves but finding talent and, and—'

'Exploiting it?' I say helpfully.

'The word I was looking for was managing,' says Sid, sternly. 'But you've got the general idea. If we take the risk then it's only right that we should take some of the profit.'

' "Some"?' I say.

'Nearly all,' says Sid. 'And we don't want to let ourselves in for too much risk either.'

'What exactly did you have in mind?' I ask.

'Park your arse.' Sid waves me towards this scruffy old leather settee that looks like fifteen feet of Hush Puppies. It's a shame really. A nice chintz cover would brighten the thing up a treat. I don't suppose Rosie has the time.

'The public are very fickle these days. You don't know which way they're going to turn. You've got to appeal to all age groups, as well. What I mean is, we can't afford to have all our eggs in one basket. I learned my lesson when I got stuck with all those bleeding hula hoops and pogo sticks.'

'What happened to them in the end, Sid?' I am always interested in news of Sidney's business ventures. It makes a change to have first hand suffering instead of all the stuff you read about in the papers.

'I sold most of them off as a Christmas game. You hang up the hula hoop and chuck the pogo stick through the middle of it.'

'Sophisticated stuff, Sid.'

'Don't take the piss, Timmo. Kid's toys are far too bleeding complicated these days. All they want to do is smash things up. I got the idea for HULAPOG from Jason.'

Just in case you do not know or have forgotten, Jason is

Sidney's firstborn and as nasty a piece of work as ever smeared its jammy fingers down the inside of your trouser leg. Seven years old and dead lucky that he still has the wind left to blow out the candles on his birthday cake. There is also the infant Jerome who is the spitting image of his brother – all he does is spit.

'He's an aggressive little chap,' I say.

'Spirited is the word I would use,' says Sid. 'I wanted to talk to you about Jason. That kiddy has got charisma.'

My face falls. 'Oh, Sid. I'm sorry to hear that. Still, they can do wonders these days if they get onto things in the early stages.'

'What are you bleeding rabbiting about?' snarls Sid. 'There's nothing wrong with him. He's got star quality, that's what I was saying. He figures large in my plans.'

My heart sinks until it is practically resting on my action man kit. 'Not another David Cassidy,' I groan. 'You can't walk down the street without tripping over some spotty kid belting out golden mouldies before his balls drop.'

'Shut your face and listen,' says Sid unsympathetically. 'I want to give you the broad picture before we start going into details.'

'We're going to have broads, are we?' I say, perking up a bit.

Ever since some half-witted bird told Sid he looked like Paul Newman he has been inclined to pepper his rabbit with Americanisms.

'Are you trying to take the piss? I'm talking about the range of our activities, aren't I? We want to appeal to all sections of the public so we got to get together a variety of acts. We want a kid for the teeny boppers, a group – and one of those Hermasetas would be a good idea.'

'I don't get you, Sid. They're those little things you put in your coffee, aren't they?'

'I mean one of those blokes who looks like a bird. They're very popular, they are.'

'You mean a hermaphrodite, Sid.' Sidney tries hard with

the Sunday newspapers but when you have had most of your education off the labels on sauce bottles it is difficult not to get confused.

'All right, all right. Have it your own way, Master Mind. As long as he can hold a guitar so the thin end is pointing towards the ceiling, that's all I'm interested in.'

'Where are you going to find all this talent, Sid?'

Sid produces a large cigar and shoves it into his cake-hole. Somewhere in Central London, Lew Grade must be feeling icy fingers running up his spine.

'Quantity is no problem, Timmo. It's finding kids with the right qualifications. Dedicated, talented—'

'And prepared to work for nothing.'

Sidney shakes his head slowly. 'Somewhere along the line you've become cynical, Timmo. That's very sad.'

'Somewhere along the line I met you, Sid. Let's face it, sentiment has never blurred your business vision.'

Sid shakes his head. 'I don't know what you're on about. Look, if you're interested in seeing how I spot talent you can come with me tonight. There's a folk singer I want to have a decco at. "Rambling Jack" Snorter. He's on at a boozer in the East End.'

My ears prick up when I hear the word boozer. I don't fancy drinking at home except at Christmas.

'What about the kids? Is Rosie coming back?'

Sid looks sheepish. 'Gretchen can look after them.'

'Gretchen?'

'The au pair.'

Au pair? The words trip off the tongue like 'knocking shop', don't they? I can just see her. Blonde, blue-eyed and with a couple of knockers like Swedish cannon balls. No wonder Sid is looking embarrassed. With his record he has probably been through her more times than the Dartford tunnel.

'Don't let your imagination run riot,' sighs Sid. 'Rosie chose her. She hasn't won a lot of beauty contests.'

As if to prove his point a bird comes in with a complexion like a pebble dash chicken house. For a moment I think she is wearing a mask – when I take a good look at her I wish she was. I have seen birds with warts before – but not on their warts. I don't go a bundle on her hair either. It is like mousy candy floss, or the stuff that comes out of your Bex Bissell. One feature you can't fault her on is her knockers. They are right out of the top drawer – in fact they are so big they would fill the whole blooming chest. They certainly fill hers.

'Ah, Gretchen,' says Sid, putting on his 'Another glass of port, Lady Prendergast?' voice. 'I don't think you've met my brother-in-law?'

When I was a kiddy, I shut my digits in a car door. When Gretchen folds her mit around mine and applies 'pleased to meet you' pressure, the sensation is about the same. Strong? This girl could play centre back for Moscow Dynamo and only your shin bones would know the difference.

'Pleased to do you,' she grunts. 'How do you meet?'

'Gretchen is learning English at Clapham Junction College of Commerce,' says Sid, chattily.

I nod agreeably while I try and rub the circulation back into my pinkies and Sid explains about us nipping out for a few jars.

Funny how first impressions can be misleading sometimes.

'Must be a strain to control yourself, when you've got that about,' I say as we scamper down the steps.

'Yeah. I nearly swung for her a couple of times,' says Sid. 'She cooked us a stew once. I think she made it from old shaving brushes. Talk about diabolical. The cat took one look at it and ran up the chimney. We had a fire in the grate at the time, too.'

Sid still has his Rover 2000 and I feel like Lord Muck as I settle back against the leather and watch the Thames twinkling away like the froth on a pool of piss.

'We should have time to catch Rambling Jack and have

a decko at one of Rosie's places,' says Sid. 'You know the East End at all, do you?'

I don't really and it doesn't look as if I am going to get the chance because they seem to be pulling it down even faster than the part of London I am living in.

'Some right villains hang out around here,' says Sid. 'Mind how you go when you get the first round in.'

I reckon if Sid made a million you would still think he had fish hooks sewn to the insides of his pockets.

The Prospect of Ruin is packed out with everyone from candidates for 'The Upper Class Twit Of The Year' award to blokes who look as if they taught Bill Sykes how to scowl. You would think that two different clubs had booked on the same night.

'The toffs come here because they fancy a bit of slumming,' says Sid. 'It's the nearest most of them ever get to villainy until they join the stock exchange.'

'Creme de menthe frappé and a packet of crisps?' I say as I push my way into the crowd round the bar. Sid's reply is not the kind of thing I would like to quote in a book that might find its way into the hands of minors – or even miners for that matter, and does not stay in my mind long. The reason? I find myself face to face with a really knockout bint. She is dead class. You can tell that by the string of pearls round her neck and the little pink flushes that light up her alabaster shoulder blades.

'I'm sorry,' I say as I go out of my way to brush past her. 'There's a bit of a crush in here.'

'That's quite all right.' Her voice goes up like the cost of living and she turns a few shades pinker.

'Are you on your tod?' I say. I mean, it's favourite to ask isn't it? You don't want to lash out on a babycham and find that there is some geezer with her.

'I'm with friends,' she says, very dainty like. I take a gander and see another filly and a couple of blokes who look as if their stiff white collars do up on their adam's apples.

'Be presumptuous of me to offer you a drink then, wouldn't it?' I often chuck in a long word like that because it shows an upper class bird that there is more to me than meets the thigh. I may not speak very proper but I have a way with me – I have it away with me too, sometimes, but that is another story.

'Are you a waterman?' says the bird, with a trace of interest.

'Only when all the beer has run out,' I say, wondering what she is on about.

'Eewh.' I don't know if that is how you spell it but it sounds something like that. It is the kind of noise the Queen Mother would make if she found you wiping the front of your jeans with one of the corgis.

'Daffers!'

The voice belongs to a herbert with a mug built round his hooter. Daffers makes another uncomfortable noise and pads off.

I get the beers in and join Sid.

'You'll never get anywhere with her, mate,' he says gloomily. 'Apart from the fact that she probably finds you repulsive, she's not going to blot her meal ticket.'

'I don't know so much.' Daffers keeps shooting glances at me and experience has taught me that where there is life there is poke. 'When are we going to see old Rumbling Tum?' I ask.

Sid does not have to answer because a bloke with a red velvet jacket appears on a small stage and grabs a microphone.

'Good evening, ladies and gentlemen, and welcome to the Doom. Tonight we're very fortunate to have a return visit from that popular son of the sod—'

His voice drones on but I find myself concentrating on a geezer with a big black beard who is clearly pissed out of his mind. He is barging into tables and cursing and muttering fit to kit out a TV comedy series. I don't know why they haven't chucked him out.

'Do us a favour, Timmo. I don't want to miss any of this.' Sid shoves his empty glass into my hand and I am fighting my way back to the bar again. Blooming marvellous, isn't it? Working with Sid is always the same. The outlay is more guaranteed than the return.

Daffers has not pressed forward with the rest of her mates and I can see her trying to think of something to say. That makes two of us.

'You look like an 'ore,' she says.

For a moment I cannot believe my ears. She looks such a nice girl too. What a thing to say. No bird has ever spoken to me like that before.

'Nobody's perfect,' I say. Maybe it is the diamante on the lapels of my shirt. Mum thought it was a bit much.

'I thought Thames Tradesmen were awfully unlucky at Henley.'

Now she has really lost me. What is she on about?

'I'm in the entertainment business,' I say. 'Do you fancy something?'

'I think I've had enough already.'

'Force yourself.'

'Well, a glass of white wine, please.'

Sidney must be right. They are all at it. And it costs as much as a pint of bitter, too. Diabolical!

'"And the brave young sons of Eireann came pouring through the door. And the snivelling British Tommies fell grovelling on the floor."' I turn round and – blooming heck! The bearded git must be Rambling Jack Snorter. His accent is as thick as an upright shillelah and the first three rows are reeling under a hail of spittle.

I tear myself from Daffer's side and return to Sid.

'What do you think?' he says.

'He's all right if you've got an umbrella,' I say. 'Does he always go in for this anti-British stuff?'

'He's very committed,' says Sid.

'And frequently, too, I should reckon,' I venture. 'I think he comes on a bit strong, myself.'

'He's controversial I'll grant you,' says Sid. 'But that's a good thing these days. He can create a dialogue between himself and the audience.'

'You mean, like that bloke who just threw a bottle at him and told him to piss off back to Ireland?'

'That kind of thing, Timmo.' Sid grabs me by the arm and steers me away from the stage. 'I think we might see if his voice carries.'

'Good thinking, Sid.'

' "So here's to all brave Irishman, God bless their sparkling eyes. And hatred to the English filth whom all true men despise." '

'I like the idea of the fiddle,' I say.

'Yeah. But they break easily, don't they?'

'They do if that one is anything to go by. Does he always finish his act by being thrown out of one of the windows?'

'Not usually,' says Sid, ducking. 'It's just that some of these dockers are a bit touchy. They're big men but very sensitive. Do you fancy another beer?'

'I don't think we're going to be able to get one, Sid. That's the governor draped over the partition, isn't it?'

'You're right. It's a lively little place, no doubt about it. I must come again some time.'

'Give them a couple of years to rebuild.' I duck as another bottle shatters against the wall above my head. If we keep under the table and push it towards the door we may be all right.'

Sid nods and turns up the collar of his jacket. 'Yeah, I don't like leaving the car for too long around here. Last time I was in the neighbourhood the kids were playing tiddly winks with hub-caps. Some little bleeder whipped my aerial. It wouldn't have been so bad but I was doing forty miles an hour at the time.

Daffers is sheltering under a nearby table and I nod to her as we crawl past. 'Super to meet you,' she says. 'Good luck with the rowing.'

'What was she on about?' says Sid. 'What have you been telling her?'

'Search me. I think she's a bit touched.'

'I wouldn't mind touching her and all. Lovely the way her bristols were hanging down like that.'

The sight has not been lost on me and I would be very willing to show the lady that what I don't know about rowing I know about in and out. I mean, it's practically the same thing, isn't it? Women on their hands and knees are always a favourite with me. A bit of dangle and a nice inviting curve to the backside – Down Lea!

We get to the car just as the fire engine comes round the corner and nearly collides with the first of the police cars.

'Lovely publicity,' says Sid, enviously. 'It's a shame we don't have him under contract.'

'Sign him up and you'll have us all under six feet of earth,' I say. 'He's a raving nutter, that bloke.'

'He's outrageous,' agrees Sid. 'But that's what a section of the market wants, these days. I wonder if I could get him to wear drag and dye his hair purple.'

Sid rambles on in this vein until he informs me that we are approaching Plonkers.

'Yeah. Diabolical name, isn't it? I told her people would associate it with bonkers and she said that was the idea.'

The place is down Fulham way and there are a load of high class wheels parked outside the front door. All lean and hunched-up like greyhounds crapping in the gutter. Inside there is a long bar and lots of alcoves and small tables. There is sawdust on the floor and a few geezers wearing striped aprons who cater for the wine-drinking public. I have to admit that quite a few members of the grape-group are present and they make a marked contrast to the regulars at The Prospect of Doom. Some of them are even wearing suits and the whine of their upper class rabbit would drill holes in the side of a battleship.

If Rosie is glad to see us, the fact is not communicated by any movement of her features.

'Oh, you've come,' she says.

'Only metaphysically,' says Sid for some reason that I find hard to explain.

'What can I offer you to drink?' says Rosie, all posh-like.

'I'll have a glass of the house white,' says Sid.

'I'll try the pillar box red,' I say.

Once again Rosie's features do not spring into smile position with whippet-like swiftness. 'Don't treat the place like the public bar at the Highwayman,' she says coldly.

And to think I can remember when she used to believe that the sun set every time Sid fastened his pyjama cord. Some birds go off faster than last year's turkey.

I turn away from this timely warning to anyone considering getting nuptially knotted and take a butchers round the room. Imagine my surprise – go on, please do – when I see Daffers and the bloke she was with, sitting in one of the alcoves. I can recognise him by the black eye and the lump on the top of his nut – he went out of the window just after Rambling Jack Snorter.

Daffers recognises me the instant our mince-pies meet and I hear the familiar strains of the love theme from Chaik's *Romeo and Juliet* bashing a hole in my lug holes – with the last tinkling notes running away down the front of my Y-fronts. Surely fate must have thrown us together? Daffers clearly thinks so. She scampers to my side and informs me that Algie is on the point of passing out. A combination of booze and amateur brain surgery has reduced his already sub-standard sex appeal to vanishing point.

'I think he ought to go home,' she murmurs. 'He's not himself.'

I am tempted to suggest that any change must be an improvement but I control myself.

'You have beautiful eyes,' I say as if nothing in the world could make me think about anything else.

'You mustn't say that.' Daffers squeezes my arm and her fate is sealed. Once birds start touching you it is but a question of minutes before their knickers are spoiling the cut of your jacket pocket.

'Where does he live?'

'Just round the corner, but he's in no state to drive.'

'I'll drive.' The words pop out of my mouth so fast that I think someone else must have said them.

'Would you really?'

I knock back the red plonk so as not to offend Rosie and tell Sid that I am popping out for a few minutes.

'Blimey, you're a sucker for failure, aren't you?' he says. 'Don't hang about. I don't want to stay here all night.'

I ignore him and help steer Algie out of the door. There is a glow in the east which makes me wonder if The Prospect of Doom is still burning. Algie has one of those little sports cars with about enough room in the back seat to lay a sausage roll lengthways and it is like fitting a broken umbrella into a shoe box to get him stowed away.

'You should have gone in the back, really,' I say. 'Still, I'm glad you didn't.'

Daffers pulls her skirt down towards her knees and runs her hand up my forearm. 'Third on the left and I'll give you instructions from there.'

'Filthy Irish swine,' drones Algie's voice from the back seat. His head drops back and he begins to snore loudly.

'Do you think we're going to be able to get him out?' murmurs my new friend. For some reason best known to herself her words accompany the pressure of dainty finger tips against my upper thigh.

'No trouble,' I breathe. 'Now, tell me. How do you get this thing into gear?'

A few thousand fumbles later, we have arrived in a narrow cobbled mews which Daffers informs me is where Algie lives. I would have thought he could have done better than to kip over a garage but I don't say anything. There is no point in hurting people's feelings, is there? Not that Algie would speak up if I gave him a lantern slide lecture on the Kama Sutra. He is definitely out for the count. I, on the other hand am now definitely out for something one letter shorter.

'What are we going to do?' Daffer's concern sounds about as genuine as that of a bloke watching his mother-in-law drive over the side of a cliff.

'I think it might be best to leave him here, don't you?' I gaze into the bird's eyes and give a little shudder like a twig snatched away by a dangerous current over which it has no control.

'Yes.' The word urges her lips a few dangerous inches closer to mine and she shares my shiver.

'Mmmm,' I say. The noise savours the pleasures to come and the last 'm' accompanies the arrival of my north and south against Daffer's soft, warm lips. At the same instant my right hand glides smoothly but purposefully between the lady's thighs. She stiffens for a minute and then relaxes, sliding her arms round my neck.

'Naughty,' she says approvingly.

I don't rush things but gently chew her lips whilst brushing my fingers against the fragile fabric guarding the entrance to her spasm chasm. At basement level percy is rolling out like a fireman's hose and I have to effect a quick readjustment of my threads in order to rearrange the accommodation. Daffers is not slow to diagnose my problem and her thoughtful fingers arrive like a batch of flying doctors. As I hook my pinkies under the rim of her panties her own digits ease down my zipper and prepare to take percy for walkies.

We are now profitably involved in two areas of mutual interest and as our fingers glide and caress a certain urgency invades our actions. I slide my hand under Daffers' back bumpers and with a little help from my friend tug her knicks towards an appointment with the carpet pile. For her part, Daffers is equally swift to expose my parts and percy soars upward like a twenty five pounder field gun released from its camouflage netting.

'We mustn't!' gasps Daffers, eagerly. Even if your only

experience of birds is helping old ladies across the road you soon get to realise that the hot flushes often coincide with the cold feet. They don't mean it, of course, but a word of reassurance is always appreciated.

'You're beautiful,' I breathe. Not the most original words in the English language but they pull more birds than a fleet of tugs. The steam is now running down the inside of the windows and it joins my impulsive lips in drowning any more of Daffers' half hearted objections. I settle back into my seat and pull my passionate playmate towards me. With encouraging haste she scrambles across my knees and suddenly the car is a very small place. In the circumstances the best thing to do seems to be to make use of every inch of space and I slot into Daffers with a speed that would bring tears to the eyes of any woodwork master in the country. My hands close about her back buffers and we thump happily while I watch the misty outlines in the mews rise and fall in time with the car springs.

'Heaven!' breathes my new friend. 'Oh, it's good.'

I am in no mood to disagree with her and as the warm currents stirring through my loins race towards the rapids I sense that a small weight loss in the Y-front area is imminent if not even nearer.

'What the Devil!'

That didn't sound like me? And it's not the kind of thing I say.

'What the hell are you doing, Daffers?!'

With a sense of extreme irritation I realise that Algie has woken up. Some people have no feelings, do they? What a minute to choose. Just when I'm—

'A-a-a-a-a-a-'

'Daffers! You swine!'

'-a-a-a-a-a-gh-!'

I stretch out an arm for the door handle and – oh dear! – stand by for another Lea Golden Rule: always leave the vehicle in gear when you're having feels on wheels. That way you avoid releasing the hand brake and rolling backwards into all those dustbins. What a good job I had just put down a deposit, otherwise there might have been a nasty accident. Terrible to be snapped off in your prime.

'Take that, you—!'

Algie is obviously feeling much stronger and I think it is probably safe to leave him and Daffers to sort things out. I open the door and fall into a sea of bottles – well, it is difficult to be light on your feet when your trousers are round your ankles and you have got some bloke thumping you in the ear hole.

They do all right for themselves in this mews, I can tell you. The contents of all the dustbins scattered about would stock a boozer.

'What the Devil—!?'

This time it is a geezer leaning out of a window. He is probably fretting because Algie's sharp little motor car has dug itself into his front door. I am feeling decidedly fragile at knee level and am grateful that Plonkers is only just round the corner. Even a glass of red wine will go down a treat in my condition. I am but a few feet from the door when a human body emerges from it at an angle of forty-five degrees. This trajectory is maintained for about six feet and then the body descends sharply into the gutter. By the cringe, but it is a night for violence, isn't it? It is amazing that anyone dares to step out for a drink these days. No doubt some undesirable scruff is being given the bum's rush from Rosie's posh clip joint.

In a manner of speaking I am correct. The stream of filthy lingo rising from the gutter could issue from only one cakehole.

'What happened, Sid?' I say, seizing the arm which is swinging back into punch-up position.

'No bugger talks to my old woman like that and gets away with it.' Sid surges towards the door but I manage to hold him back.

'What did he say?'

'He said he was going to liaise with her the weekend he got back from Amsterdam. Imagine that. He's hardly through the door and he's off with someone's wife. I bet he's got some lovely kiddies at home, too.'

'Liaise isn't a place, you berk,' I say helpfully. 'It means to get in touch with someone.'

'Oh dear,' says Sid. 'Are you sure? No wonder Rosie got so worked up.'

'What did you do?'

Sid looks down at the pavement. 'I punched him about a bit. Nothing too strenuous. It was only when they all went for me that I had to defend myself.' Before he can say anything else I hear the shrill note of an ambulance approaching at speed. I do not have to consult my crystal ball to know where it is going.

'I think we'd better get out of here,' I say. 'I don't reckon it's one of our evenings. Not unless you fancy our chances of finding a load of talent in the local nick.'

Sid thinks hard for a minute. 'It's a nice publicity gimmick,' he says slowly. Poor old Sid. If the Indians gave him beads he would be grateful.

'Come on!' I say. 'Take me home, I'm knackered.'

'You can stay with us,' says Sid. 'There's loads of room and we can talk about the proposition in the morning.'

'Is that going to be all right with Rosie?'

Sid says words to the effect that he is not going to be over-worried whether it is all right with Rosie or not. Furthermore, that if Rosie does not like it she knows what she can do with herself. It is obviously a subject that Sid enjoys talking about and he is still going strong when we get back to trendy Vauxhall.

'Fancy a night cap?' he says advancing to the booze tray. I refuse and am directed to the third floor while my brother-in-law fixes himself another large scotch. He drinks too much, there is no doubt about it.

I am feeling dead knackered and the prospect of a bit of kip is very welcome. It has been a day rich in experience if not in achievement and I will have much to think about before the sand man dusts my mince pies with – knickers! For some reason the light in the room Sid directed me to is not working. Not to worry, I will do something about it in the morning.

I feel my way to the bed and start to strip off. I will have to sleep in the buff but that is no hardship. A bit chilly to start off with but – that's funny. It seems quite warm as I slide a leg inside. Warm as the hand that grabs my action man kit.

'Mr. Noggett. You naughty man!' The voice is full of East European promise and is not unknown to me.

'I'm sorry,' I squeak – and I mean squeak. 'It's not Mr. Noggett. It's me. I thought this was my room.'

'Is my room. Everything in it is mine.' Something about the way she says that makes me fear the worst – that and the way her mit is still anchored to my hampton like it is a try your strength machine.

'I'll go.'

'No! You come here for hanky wanky. You no need to be ashamed. It is always the same at the time of the potato harvest in my homeland.' So that is where she gets her grip from. 'The young men drink the Spudovitch and make merry with the maidens in the cow byres.'

'Fascinating,' I murmur. 'I've often been tempted by those Winter Break holidays.'

'Introduce me to your friend.' Gretchen's tone suggests that the time for cocktail party banter has passed.

'I must go.'

'No!! My body will not be denied. Enter me!'

I would enter her for the Smithfield Show tomorrow but that is about all. Unfortunately she must have been taught unarmed combat at her mother's knee and my left arm is forced up my back towards the nape of my neck before you can say Siberia.

'Make frisky with me.'

If only I could remember what she looked like with the light on.

'Maybe you like to make love with light on?'

'No!' Now it is my turn to bash the negatives. The sight of that face at a moment like this could put the kibosh on my sex life for keeps.

'You like big titties?' Gretchen pulls my face down onto her barrage balloon bosom and at that moment a flicker of lust passes through my action man kit. Never one of the smartest J.T.s in the business my spam ram responds with animal urgency to the presence of sheer brute size.

'Is good, no?'

The obvious answer to that question is no. However an even more obvious answer has presented itself to me. The only way to get rid of the iron maiden is going to be to give in to her. Moving my head slightly so that I will be able to perform the vital movements whilst still alive, I hum 'Rule Britannia' under my breath and give brave, foolhardy percy his head. It may not be the end to a perfect day but at least it is the end.

CHAPTER TWO

In which an attempt is made to turn nephew, Jason Noggett, into a six-year-old Mick Jagger and Timmy shares a few idyllic moments with lonely Mrs Blenkinsop.

'I'd forgotten she was in the spare room,' says Sid.

'Forgotten! ? Blooming heck! She could have killed me. When she fell asleep on top of me it took me ten minutes to crawl out.'

Sid waves my complaints away and continues to clean his earhole with a teaspoon.

'Don't worry about it. It's all part of life's rich tapioca, water that's been passed under the bridge. Clear your mind and start thinking about Noggo Enterprises.'

'Noggo Enterprises? What's that?'

'That's us, Timmo. The company that's going to promote all this talent under the Bella label.'

I politely refuse Gretchen's offer of a second helping of porridge and put down my knife and fork – well, it is that lumpy you have to eat it with a knife and fork. At first I thought she had dropped a few spuds in it.

'Why "Bella"?' I say.

'It's an anadin of label,' says Sid proudly.

'I don't see what that's got to do with it. "Raft" is an anagram of "Fart" but I wouldn't use it as a name for an air freshener.'

As usual, Sid is slow to admit that I have a point. 'In the world of entertainment, presentation is half the battle. You've got to be slick and with it.' Sid scrapes egg off the front of his shirt and licks the knife.

'O.K., Sid. You're the boss. Where do we start?'

'Right here in this house. You must have noticed that young Jason is not with us?'

'He hasn't run away from home?' I try hard to keep a

note of delirious gaiety out of my voice but it is not easy.

'Do you know how old he is?'

I pretend to give the question a lot of thought. 'Let me see. You and Rosie have been married for nearly six years, so he must be about six and a half.'

Sidney's face darkens beneath the stubble. 'Watch it, Timmo. Just because he was a bit premature, there's no need to go jumping to conclusions.'

'Premature? He was so early he was practically singing at the bleeding wedding.'

'I won't tell you again, Timothy. The child is a mature six and very advanced for his age, considering everything. I believe he can open up a whole new child market for us. I've sent him upstairs to get his clobber on.'

'Surely he's too young, Sid?'

'Not these days he isn't. The kids are the ones buying most of the records and the real mini-groovers don't have anyone to identify with. If we can launch Jason we make our own market.'

When Sid talks like that I find it difficult to understand why everything we touch loses money. It seems such a good idea, doesn't it?

'Here I am, Dad.'

Blimey! The little basket looks like an explosion in a sequin factory. Faced with that kind of competition Gary Glitter might as well get a job as a bank clerk.

'Can he play that thing?' I am referring to the kidney-shaped guitar with more sharp corners than a lorry-load of hair pins.

'He can strum it a bit. The backing group will supply all the noise.'

'Jason and the Golden Fleas,' I say wittily.

'Uncle Timmy, stupid,' says the only kid in south London to be given a new set of nappies for his fourth birthday.

'Sing him our song,' encourages Sid.

I compose my features to receive the worst and, as usual, get it:

'Stomp on your momma,
Stomp on your pa,
Stomp on everybody
With a yah, yah!'

'It sounds better with his guitar plugged in,' says Sid. My first instinct is to say that I would prefer it with the little bleeder's finger jammed up a light socket but I control myself. Criticism is always better received if it is constructive.

'It's a bit violent, isn't it?' I ask.

Sid takes another swig of tea and wipes his mouth with the back of his hand.

'Exactly, Timmo. That's what we in the business call the difference factor. You take all the kids singing at the moment. Not only are they older than Jason but they're all singing ballads. I see Jason as the first of the mini-bopper neo-decadents.'

'Yerwhat?'

'A seven-year-old Mick Jagger.'

It takes me a few moments to come to terms with this idea but when I see the pout on Jason's thick little lips – not as thick as they would be if I had my way – I begin to get Sid's drift.

'Blimey!'

'Yeah. You remember how The Stones made The Beatles look like a load of fairies? Well, Jason is going to make David Cassidy and Donny Osmond look like Hansel and Gretel.'

'My best friend called Gretel,' interrupts Gretchen who has appeared with a plate of charcoal doorsteps which might once have been bread. 'You like her. She big girl.'

'Belt up, shagnasty,' says Sid, unkindly. 'Why don't you push off and put the porridge through the mincer?'

Gretchen must be doing badly at the Clapham Junction College of Commerce because she smiles happily and bears the vat of porridge away humming what sounds like an old Slobovian sea shanty.

'I think your mother must have taught her to cook,' says Sid wearily. 'She works on the principle that the quickest way to a man's fart is through his stomach.'

'Very funny, Sid,' I say, humouring him. 'But do you really think that the market is right for a hard rocking seven-year-old?'

'He'll come right through to the mini-market,' says Sid. 'He speaks their language. He is one of them. Not a manufactured product forced on them by their mums and dads.'

'He's a manufactured product forced on them by us.'

'Exactly, Timmo. That's the important difference. He's a rallying standard in the battle against parental conformity. The leader of the mini-bopper rebellion.'

I look at Jason who has one finger wedged up his hooter and is stirring circles in the sugar bowl with another and ask myself: can Sid be right this time? It is obvious that he has been getting ideas from the magazines in Doctor Naipaul's waiting room but that has never been a guarantee of success in the past.

'I'm still sceptical, Sid,' I say.

'Well, you'd better go and see a doctor,' says Sid, screwing up his eyes in distaste. 'Don't talk about it at the breakfast table. It puts me right off my kipper.'

'No, Sid,' I say wearily. 'I meant that I'm not convinced you're right.'

Sid stands up, 'You don't have to take my word for it. I've entered Jason for the vicar's kiddies talent contest. You wait till you see what he does to them down there. It'll be an ideal test run. After that it's the big time. Eh, Show Stopper?'

Jason tries to nod but his finger is still up his hooter and he nearly does himself a nasty injury.

'What are you going to call him, Sid?'

Sidney switches on his 'I'm so clever I might kill myself' expression.

'Plain Jason,' he says.

'I don't get it,' I say. 'I mean, he is plain but do you want to remind every—'

'If you weren't so stupid I would think you were taking the piss,' says Sid.

'Uncle Timmy, very stupid,' says Jason.

'What I meant—' Sid hits every word like it is a nail. 'What I meant is that we are going to call him Jason. Jason all by itself. Jason nothing. It's his real name, see? Very natural, very genuine. It's a wonderful gimmick.'

'I prefer Jason Nothing,' I say.

Sid controls himself with difficulty. 'You keep your preferences to yourself and help Jason off with his suit. I'm going to see about a group that could be very big. If I'm not back by four you'll have to take Jason down to the church hall. And check that the sockets fit the plug on his guitar. They've got some terrible old stuff down there.'

Marvellous, isn't it? With all my looks and personality I end up as dresser to a six-year-old kid whose nose runs faster than a Derby winner. I would not mind so much if Jason was not such an unco-operative little basket. He refuses to change at the church hall and throws a paddy because two of his sequins fall off coming down the stairs. Rosie is out on business so I have to sew the bleeding things on. I have just finished doing this when Jason wants to do potty and I find out I have sewn his trousers to his pants. This piece of information costs me another five sequins and twenty minutes during which my lips are jammed together tighter than a novice nun's knees at an Irish funeral party.

By the time I have finished it is a race against time to get to the church hall before the vicar's frolic starts.

'Uncle Timmy catch it when my dadda gets back,' says Jason happily.

'Little Jason catch a bunch of fives up his bracket if he

doesn't button his lip,' I hiss. 'Now, get a move on or we're going to miss the bus.'

You would not believe it, but the little basket has the gall to throw a tantrum because he is not travelling by chauffeur-driven Rolls. God knows what Sidney has been telling him. I feel a right berk standing in the bus queue with Jason in his ridiculous clobber. He makes a toreador look like one of those skin heads who wanders down Oxford Street chanting 'Hairy Krisnan'.

The bus conductor is not over-thrilled to see him either.

'You going to bring the organ on as well, mate?' he says to me. 'You can take him on top if you like. There's an old girl up there with a bunch of bananas.'

I ignore these crude attempts at humour and try to avoid the other passengers' eyes as I cradle Jason's guitar on my lap. He may be the answer to every five-year-old's prayers but he is not doing much for the senior citizens huddled around me. They watch him like snakes being offered a glass rat for dinner. The Vicar does not exactly cream his cassock either.

'I'm afraid the fancy dress party was last week,' he says, nervously.

'Belt him, Uncle Timmy,' says Jason in a loud whisper.

'This talented little chap is taking part in your contest, Vicar,' I say evenly. 'I'm sorry we're a few minutes late.'

'Jason Noggett, is it?' says the Vic. going down his list.

'I don't think I've seen you or your wife since the wedding.'

'I'm not married,' I say.

The Fire Escape's face clouds over. 'Oh dear. I'm afraid that only those relationships that have been sanctified by the Holy Sacrament can offer up their fruit for inclusion in our talent contest.'

For a moment I think he is talking about a vegetable show and then I get his drift. 'I'm the boy's uncle,' I say.

The Vicar looks much happier. 'Of course. How silly of me. It's so easy to jump to conclusions these days, isn't it?'

'How long before he goes on?' I ask. I never feel comfortable talking to holy men. I think it goes back to when I was a kiddy and could not understand why they were dressed up as birds.

'He'll have to go on right at the end,' says the Vic. 'I've made out a list and I can't change it now.'

'Top of the bill,' says Junior Monster, showing the first signs of pleasure he has evinced all afternoon.

'It's all harmless fun,' says the man of God realising that he has got 'star or bust' material on his hands. 'Nothing too serious. I got the idea from one of those television programmes.'

I am getting ideas myself, but from a different quarter. One of the ladies present, presumably a Mum, is definitely in the knock-out class. Slim, but with nice knockers and a wistful expression that makes me want to defend her against dragons and people like me. She has her arm resting on the shoulder of a kid wearing specs and long velvet shorts. The kid looks terrified, maybe because he is scared that his cello is going to fall on top of him. He holds his bow like a character in a fairy story defending himself against a giant spider. Poor little sod. He has obviously got no chance in the competition and is scared to wetsville about going on the stage.

I catch mum's eye just as the Vic. hurries off to investigate a reported stabbing in the ladies – I noticed a geezer frisking the kids for weapons as I came through the door.

'Have a shufti at the opposition, Jason boy,' I say giving my tiny charge a gentle push in the direction of the stage, '– and don't use language like that in the church hall!' It may have been a silly place to leave a pile of hassocks but there was no need for him to say that. I don't know where the little bastard gets it from.

'Kids today!' I say in my best 'over the garden wall' manner. 'Little devils, aren't they?'

'There's a lot of high spirits about,' says Pablo Casals's mother. She has one of those posh voices that suggests she lives in one of the houses facing Clapham Common. We live in a house that overlooks Clapham Common – completely.

'When's your boy going on?' I ask.

'Right at the end. It's very nerve racking, isn't it, William?' William gulps and nods miserably. It's a shame really. She should never have brought him. I know these upper class birds. They reckon they ought to get involved in the community and go around forming committees and parent teachers' associations. Their kids go to state schools and their husbands hand out glasses of sherry and talk about community spirit. When the value of their house has trebled they sell up, move to Hampstead and send the kids to public school. They do a nice tea, though.

There is a burst of jeers and whistles from behind a curtain and a kid runs past wearing a bow tie and a top hat. He is in tears and is closely followed by a mother figure.

'They did *what* with your balls?' I hear her saying as they disappear from sight.

I take a peep through the curtain and – blimey! – I am glad I don't have to go out there. They make the average Crackerjack audience look like Parkhurst lifers. I can hardly see beyond the first three rows for the pall of smoke and the kids are hopping about like a flea circus on acid. The stage is littered with orange peel and coke cans and the Vic. is waving his arms about like it is the first heat of a semaphore contest.

'Children, I appeal to you!' he shrieks.

'No you don't, Baldy! Push off!'

'What a load of rubbish!'

'Why are we waiting!'

I step back from the curtain and shoot a quick glance at Jason – I would prefer to shoot a bullet but you can't have everything you want in life. If the little bleeder can't get this lot going he might as well jack it in immediately. I hope the Vic. has the hall insured.

'William Blenkinsop, William Blenkinsop! If I'd have known Miss Trimble's mother was having her varicose veins done today I'd have put the whole thing off for a week.'

The poor old Vic. is clearly going to pieces faster than flaky cod. William Blenkinsop has turned the colour of cold suet and is led out onto the stage by his mother carrying a chair. A chorus of wolf whistles suggests that some of the kiddies present have very mature tastes. I even think I hear a shout of 'get 'em orf!' but it must be my imagination.

'What is first prize?' Jason's evil little eyes glint with anticipation. He obviously reckons it is all over bar the shouting.

'Quite an ordeal for the boy, Mrs Blenkinsop,' I say in my best Dixon of Dock Green voice.

'Yes. I wish – perhaps I shouldn't – oh, I don't know.' She leans forward nervously and I gaze sympathetically at the soft swellings in her fisherman-knit sweater. I wonder if I slid my arms round her and – no, it probably wouldn't. People have such different ideas when it comes to offering comfort.

'William Blenkinsop is going to play—' There is an ugly pause while it occurs to everyone that the Vic. has no idea what W.B. is going to play.

'With his willy!' shouts a child with a big future on late night chat shows. I can feel the glow of the Vic.'s cheeks from where I am standing. He mouths desperately into the wings.

'Bach.'

'Woof, woof!' bays the audience.

Mrs Blenkinsop stiffens beside me and for a moment I think she is going to dash on the stage and yank William off. I have not heard a worse reception since Dad played us the last wireless he nicked from the lost property office.

'Poor kid,' I breathe as William licks his lips and prepares to play the first few chords. His eyes are closed and it is only the movement of the bow that tells us he is wanging away. The row is so great you can't hear anything. Then, slowly, the music starts coming through. I don't know a cello from a pregnant fiddle but it is obvious that the kid knows how to play the thing. The audience stop giving him the bird and start to listen. By the time the last note has wafted away into the rafters you could hear a pin drop. There is a moment's pause and then lughole-shattering applause.

The only person not clapping is Jason. He looks about as happy as Ted Heath at a miners' rally.

Out on the stage, William Blenkinsop bows stiffly and walks towards his highly chuffed mum.

'O.K. Super Star,' I say to Jason. 'Now's your chance to make history. Get out there and sock it to them.' I take a last look at him and, of course, the stupid little basket has forgotten to do up his zipper. I give it a savage tug and – oh dear! The whole thing comes away in my hand.

'What you doing!?' shrieks Jason.

'It doesn't matter. You're all right. Get out there. I'll plug you in.' His trousers are very tight and nobody would recognise his willy wonker if he painted it in day glo paint.

The Vic. bustles up looking a shade happier. 'Jason Noggett, isn't it?'

'Just Jason.'

'And he's doing an impression of someone?'

'No, he's being himself,' I say. 'He's going to sing an original composition entitled "Stomp on your momma".'

The Vic. does not look as if this is the best news he has had since the second coming but nods and shambles onto the stage with his silent lips rehearsing the words to come. We follow him.

I have sussed out a power point and I plug in Jason's instrument – yes, the same thought was running through my mind – while the Vic. introduces him as Justin Jason. The little monster's reception has been mixed. A few cheers but quite a lot of whistles and raspberries. It is going to be an effort for these kids to applaud two acts in a row.

'—who is going to perform a work entitled "Stomp" – er – who is going to sing for us.'

Jason tries to come in the minute the Vic. turns to leave the stage, but unfortunately, the holy man blunders into the guitar flex. There is a blinding flash and Jason's trousers fall down. This is not the hallmark of professional class and the audience are swift to notice it. There are shrieks of unkind laughter and one or two kids are literally rolling in the aisles. Jason chucks his guitar on the ground and immediately the power point jumps out of the wall and there is a dense cloud of smoke.

'Evacuate the hall!' shrieks the Vic.

Jason tries to pull up his trousers and is hopping from the stage when I grab him. As we plunge through the curtains I can hear a noise like a herd of elephants charging through a matchbox factory.

'My dad going to smash Uncle Timmy's face in!' hisses the little viper. For two pins I would send him back to pick up his guitar but being electrocuted seems too easy a way for him to die.

As it turns out it is not Sid that I have to worry about. When I get into the wings Rosie races up to me like she has been pushed down a hill on roller skates.

'What have you done to my baby?' she shrieks.

'We had a little accident,' I say. 'It wasn't my fault. The Vicar—'

'He pulled out the front of my trousers,' interrupts Jason.

'The Vicar pulled out the front of your trousers!?' Rosie's eyes widen and I can see her mind jumping to some disturbing conclusions.

'No. He did.' Jason jabs his finger at me.

'I was trying to pull his zip. Don't go on about it, everyone is looking at me.'

Rosie is not in a forgiving mood. 'You bastard!' she

says. 'Making a laughing stock of a little kiddy. There, there, Jason darling. Mummy's here. Don't cry.'

I am surprised that the little basket has held back on the water works until now. 'Uncle Timmy say he going to hurt Jason,' he sobs.

'Right,' says Rosie. 'That's it. The child is coming with me. I knew he should have stuck with his ballet classes. I'm never going to let him into your clutches again. You'd exploit a dumb animal, let alone an innocent little boy.'

I have a point of view on the subject I would like to express but before I can open my cakehole Rosie has swept out dragging Jason behind her. He gives me a V sign just before he gets to the door.

I am considering the five ways I would most like to swing for him when there is a loud shriek from the stage. The Vic. has tried to pick up the electric guitar. Fortunately he was not standing in a bowl of water at the time. I find myself scampering to his side in the company of Mrs Blenkinsop who is also without child accompaniment. She appears to have been left holding the cello and as we ease the Vic. onto a chair I inquire after the whereabouts of the talented William.

'He went off with his father,' says Mrs B. 'You see, we're separated.' Her voice falls away like it is sliding down a mountain and immediately a great rush of sympathy sweeps down to my Y-fronts. Sad birds, helpless birds, birds with problems, they always get me going. I am probably very mixed up.

'I'm sorry,' I say.

'It doesn't matter.'

We stared at each other until the Vicar groans.

'What a disaster.' The words leak out of him as if from a perished hot water bottle.

'Don't blame yourself,' I say. 'It was probably an Act of God.' I don't know why I say that. It must have been something I picked up from a piece of Mum's karsi paper – she cuts up magazines and that kind of stuff. The Vicar stares up into the rafters and slowly nods his head.

'Perhaps,' he says after a pause.

'I didn't mean that your governor chucked a nasty at it,' I say hurriedly.

The Vic. gives one of those brave smiles that has helped make the British Empire what it is today – e.g. skint – and continues to gaze in the direction of Big G.

'A wonderful man,' says Mrs B. as we steal away leaving him mumbling about Miss Trimble and the crack in the font.

'Very dedicated,' I say. 'Tell me, how far have you got to lug that thing?'

'The cello? Oh, yes. It isn't going to be easy, is it?'

'Perhaps I can give you a hand?'

'Oh, you mustn't worry yourself about me.'

'It's no trouble.' Before she can say anything I have grabbed the merchandise and am scampering outside with it. That way she does not have any choice but to follow me.

'I'm afraid I don't have a car. Rog – my ex-husband took it.'

'That's all right,' I say, trying to hide my disappointment. 'Which way did you come?'

Ten minutes later I am holding out the fare to the same conductor who took Jason and me to the church hall.

'Put on a bit of weight, hasn't he?' he says, nodding at the cello. 'You fattening him up for Christmas?'

I restrain myself with difficulty and the rest of the journey passes with me trying to keep the cello from being kicked to pieces.

'I'll put it between my legs if you like,' says Mrs B.

The bloke in front turns round so fast he gets a crick in his neck.

'Roger usually takes William away at the weekends,' says Mrs B. as we walk along the common. 'It's amazing how empty the house feels. I look forward to having some time to myself but when I've got it I find myself just hanging around waiting for the child to come home.'

'You must have some friends,' I say.

'Not a lot. Married people seem to stick together and I don't want to sit around with a lot of divorced women discussing how their marriages broke up.' She stops outside a large semi-detached Victorian house and I can see her making up her mind whether to ask me in.

'This is where I live,' she says. 'Would you like a cup of tea or something?'

'That would be smashing,' I say, 'it's a nice house.'

'It's good to have the common so near. If you dare walk on it these days. I was followed by a man the other night.'

'I'm not surprised,' I say, willing the key into the lock.

'He stood by the gate for twenty minutes after I'd gone into the house.'

'You should have rung the police.'

The hall of the house is dark and there is a kid's bike resting against the stairs.

'I thought they'd probably tell me not to waste their time. He hadn't done anything wrong. He was probably just frustrated.' She smiles quickly and for a second I think she is going to say something else.

'There are some funny people about,' I say.

'I'm afraid the place is in a terrible mess.'

I've never met a woman who didn't say that, the minute your foot was over the threshold. When I was a window cleaner they would be apologising for everything, the furniture, the wall paper, the colour of the old man's pyjamas.

'I don't keep it too tidy on purpose. It makes it warmer, somehow.' Call me sentimental – call me Cynthia Bigboobs if it gives you a thrill – but when Mrs Blenkinsop talks like that I really feel for her – or rather, I would really like to feel for her. I reckon a bit of oggins is just what she needs to perk her up. She slips off her jacket and I make no secret of the fact that my eyes are casing her joints.

'Do you mind having it in the kitchen?'

She must be very innocent, this girl, saying things like that. 'That's quite all right,' I say.

'It's the warmest room in the house. We were about to have central heating put in when Roger found something better to do with his money.'

The kitchen is large and has a table and chairs in it. They must have knocked down a wall.

'He left you, did he?' I say.

'Yes.' A long pause. 'Yes and no. I had an affair so he had to have one. In the end his tat turned out to be bigger than my tit.' She smiles.

'That sounds funny, doesn't it?'

I nod. 'It does a bit.'

Mrs B. starts fiddling with the tea things. 'I'm always making unintentional double entendres.'

'My Mum never knows what's going to come out of the oven,' I say sympathetically.

'Y-e-s.' Mrs B. looks at me in a funny sort of way. 'Would you like a piece of cake?'

'Lovely.' It is, too, and I munch away trying to stop the crumbs building up at the corners of my north and south. That and spinach on your fangs can lose you more birds than chewing a clove of garlic.

I am not getting desperate but a certain amount of tension is building up inside me. The ice has yet to be well and truly broken and at any moment Mrs B. may suddenly leap to her feet and say 'ta' and 'ta, ta'.

'Do you still see your fellow?' I ask.

Mrs B. shakes her head. 'He went back to his wife. We have lunch occasionally but that's all.'

I take this to mean that no nooky is partaken of. Even more reason why percy should be pressed into service. Not that the hooded avenger is going to need much pressing. Down at Y-front level all systems are itching to go.

'You make a lovely cup of tea,' I say, continuing to dazzle her with verbal fireworks.

'Thank you. Would you like another piece of cake?'

'Yes, please. That's great too.' Well, they say flattery will get you anywhere, don't they?

Mrs B. sips her cup of tea and watches me and I sense that she is aware of the tensions whizzing round the room. She is fiddling with the neck of her sweater and I notice that she is wearing a ring that sparkles like an enlarged snow flake.

'That's a fantastic ring,' I say.

'Do you like it? It was my mother's.'

She stretches out her hand and I take it in mine. Choirs of angels do not burst into the Dr Zhivago theme but they might well do so. The most difficult part of getting to grips with a bird is getting to grips with her. Once you have actually touched each other everything seems much easier. That is why dancing is so much more popular than cross country running when it comes to pre-nooky exercise. Get perky percy as the filling in a body sandwich and it's Fanny Craddock to a packet of fish fingers that the frisky little fellow will be playing follow the ferret before you can say rabbit warren.

'It's lovely.'

I run my finger over the ring and down to the soft flesh between her first and second digit. Very gently, I squeeze it between finger and thumb. Mrs Blenkinsop continues to look down at the table. I take her hand in both of mine and run my fingers along the underside of her palm. Mrs Blenkinsop does not move.

'Look at me.' I tilt her head back and find that there is a tear running down one of her cheeks. I lean forward and smudge it with my lips.

'Don't cry.'

Mrs B. shakes her head slowly. 'You're going to think I'm awfully cheap.'

'No I'm not,' I say – you wouldn't expect me to say anything else, would you?

I pick up both her arms and, resting them on my shoulders, hold her close to me. She does not resist but there is no enthusiasm in any of her movements. She might be a big rag doll. I turn my head to one side and nudge her mouth into mine. I know that she wants me but I also know that she is ashamed. She is prepared to let things happen but that is all.

I push her back against the table and slide my hands up underneath the back of her skirt. She is not wearing any panties and my fingers ride on under the elastic of her tights. Mrs Blenkinsop is breathing hard and her mouth opens wider as my right hand eel-glides along her spasm chasm. Percy is now throwing himself against the side of my jeans like a whippet watching a march past of hares and I fear for the safety of my zipper mooring. If for no other reason, it is necessary for me to release the maddened spam ram. I pop Mrs B. on the edge of the table and, while her arms still loop limply round my neck, peel the tights from her legs. Hardly have they ripped over her heels than my itching fingers spring to my zipper and the mighty wurlitzah soars into glorious melody.

'No. You mustn't.' Mrs Blenkinsop's words come late and are delivered in a tone that would be pushed to prevent a boy scout dropping a sweet paper.

'Come here.' I pull Mrs B. towards me and feel the comforting touch of her thighs on either side of my hips.

The kitchen table! In many a happy year of pussy-pummelling I can never remember an occasion on which I have performed love's old sweet melody on this particular surface. Strange when one thinks of all the stories you hear.

With one hand I coax Mrs B. towards her appointment with percy while the other presses my frisky friend towards table level.

'Oh!' says Mrs B. 'Oh! O-O-O-O-H!!'

Little imagination is required to interpret the reason for these cries. I slide into Mrs B. like a hot penny into a pound of butter and the good lady shivers like a tungsten tuning fork. Talk about good vibrations, half the tea things go with the first wriggle.

Four thrusts and the lady is lying back and flexing like a shaken rope. This is the life. Happiness being spread like jam and not a drop of harm to anybody. Three cheers for little Jason and his electrifying musical talent. Without the Boy Beethoven I would not be in the pleasant position I now occupy. Percy pounds powerfully and beneath me Mrs Blenkinsop dissolves like an ice cube in a bowl of mulligatawny. Her hands come to life and are now pressed against my flexing stomach. Another tea cup falls to the floor. Oh well, that's show business. Who cares about the old woman tapping on the window pane?

The old woman tapping on the window pane? I shoot another glance over my shoulder and there she is. Bent nearly double and shielding her eyes with her hand.

Oh dear, what bad luck, as my nicely born Uncle Norm would say. This kind of thing carried to extremes could kill the sex act as early evening light entertainment.

At all costs I must protect Mrs Blenkinsop from embarrassment. She is already beginning to sense that something is interfering with my natural rhythm. Her fingers are prodding my belly button as if trying to find the switch that turns me on to full power. I check to see that the old biddy baggy is still having problems piercing the gloom and sweep Mrs B. up like a clothful of heavy crumbs. Slotted together like two parts of a cheap construction set we bundle through the kitchen door and into the hall. If Mrs B. is wondering why we are going walkies she is not complaining and as I fall to my knees on the bottom stair her arms slide round my neck and her mouth hits mine like a force ten gale.

'Oh, that was gorgeous,' she says. 'Go on!'

I don't know whether she means with the conducted tour, but at that moment an evening paper shoots through the letterbox and nearly dents my marriage prospects. I respond to the 'womp!' of the letterbox flap like a thoroughbred hearing the off and nearly disappear through the other side of the delighted Mrs B. It is not surprising that I suffer from a slight persecution complex. I mean, at any minute I expect to have to form myself into a circle as blood-crazed Indian braves storm the house. Why do I always have to share my sexual experience with at least twice the number of people that were invited?

'Go on, go on!' Mrs B. is clearly entering into the spirit of things.

It is funny how little you know about a bird until you hit the sack with her. On the other hand, what you learn in the sack can't be the whole truth either, can it? The expression on our faces changes with the angle of our bodies. (Get on with it! *Ed.*) Sorry, I get carried away, sometimes. (Don't give me ideas. *Ed.*) I wish I knew who this bloke Ed was. He would be getting a bunch of fives in the next post. The true artist is a persecuted individual in our society. Those blokes on the Guardian know what they are talking about.

Anyway, where was I? Oh yes, Hampton deep in Mrs Blenkinsop on the stairs of a large Victorian semi-detached on the edge of Clapham Common – thank you, vicar.

Fearing further interruption I flex my battered knees and set off again in search of postures new. This kind of caper could probably become very popular on the continent – I mean, long distance bicycle races, cross country skiing – why not round the house humping?

'The door on the right,' gasps Mrs B.

I blunder through it and tumble her on the bed like a sack of beautifully formed potatoes. She has what you might call a slight body and fits like a fox glove. At last we are in the traditional setting for a spot of in and out and I set out to repair our shattered rhythm with the loving attention of a craftsman restoring an old master – or possibly, young mistress.

Percy has just bashed out the opening bars of Ravel's Bolero when the phone rings. This is too much. I am not a temperamental sack artist but there are limits to the conditions I am prepared to work under. Even percy, usually about as sensitive as a cement thermometer, is beginning to respond to the flashes of nervous irritation transmitted by my uneasy mind.

'Fiddle!' Mrs B. removes the receiver and holds it to one of her shell-like ears. I hear a man's voice repeating 'Mary? Mary?' in a slightly narked fashion. A smile spreads slowly over the lady's face.

'My husband,' she whispers. 'My ex-husband.' She runs her hand down my chest and then speaks into the receiver. 'Hold on a minute, Charles.'

She places the receiver on the bedside table and slides her tickling fingers round beneath my thighs.

'Go on,' she calls softly. The smile is practically spilling over the sides of her face.

CHAPTER THREE

In which Timmy meets Nutter Normanton, the man who plays the piano with his head, and Reg, Fuggy, Pete and Trembler – fellow members of Kipper, the group Sid hopes is going to make Noggo Enterprises a fortune.

'I tell you,' says Sid. 'This group is sensational. Of course we'll have to repackage them.'

'Where did you find them?' I say.

'They were playing above a boozer in Wapping. Of course, they don't usually do that kind of thing. It was just a gig for a mate.'

'Of course.' Poor old Sid. I have seen him in this mood before. He does get so carried away. 'What are they called?'

'Bloater. One of the group comes from Yarmouth. I don't fancy it, do you?'

'I only went there once when I was a kiddy, Sid.' Sid's face shows the familiar mark of genius frustrated by incompetence.

'I don't mean Yarmouth, you berk. I mean the name of the group.'

'Oh, that. Well, I don't know really.'

'I do. Kipper.'

'I didn't know there were any,' I say, thinking I am being asked if I fancy one.

The conversation is taking place in the kitchen of the Lea mansion in Scraggs Lane, Rosie having taken umbrage in a big way over the Jason affair and ejected both Sid and myself when we limped back from our respective appointments with destiny.

Sid buries his face in his hand and groans. 'Sometimes I think you do it on purpose,' he says. 'You'd like to drive me round the twist, wouldn't you?'

'No, Sid.'

'I was not referring to the fact that one day the monotony of the grub in this bleeding hell hole might be broken by the arrival of something as unbelievably exotic as a kipper. I was putting forward a suggestion for the name of the group. What do you think of it?'

'Kipper?'

Sid nods slowly. 'That's right, Timmy. How does it grab you?'

'I like it, Sid. But aren't we moving a bit fast? What about Jason?'

'You heard your sister, Timmo. She said over her dead body. Mind you, I have thought about it but I don't think it's the right kind of publicity for the boy. We'll leave it alone for a bit and wait for her to change her mind. She'll be falling over herself when she sees the success we have with Kipper. I do wish you'd brought back that guitar, though.'

'I told you, Sid. I couldn't touch it. It was live.'

Sid bangs his fist on the table and a couple of slices of mum's toast fall on the floor and splinter into little pieces.

'They're buggers down at that music shop,' he says. 'The bloke told me it was one of the best electric guitars to come out of Hong Kong between the wars. You don't get anything for three quid these days.'

'Have you actually signed them up?' I say, deciding that it would be as well to change the subject. The papers are full of the church hall that burned down in South West London seconds after it was full of children.

'Yeah. That's the beauty of it. I was amazed how keen they were.' The minute I hear that, my blood runs colder than a penguin's chuff. Anybody who falls over themselves to sign up with Sid must be worse than useless.

'They said they were looking for a manager,' says Sid cheerfully. 'I got them dirt cheap, too. Hundred quid a week. Anything we make over that is profit.'

'A hundred quid a week!'

Sid puts on his misunderstood look. 'Well, there are five of them. I don't see what you're worrying about. You don't have to pay the bill – well, not directly.'

'What do you mean, "not directly"?' I say sharply.

'I mean, until we're established I won't be able to pay you any wages. We'll have to plough all the cash into the talent. You should be thankful I'm not charging you for the guitar.'

'I've been on the point of grateful tears for the last twenty minutes,' I say. 'Tell me, Sid. When am I going to get an eyeful of – of Kipper?'

Sid swells out his chest. 'You're going to see them in action sooner than you might think. Have you heard of the Rainbow?'

'Course I have, Sid. You don't mean—?'

'Two streets away there's a roller skating rink that has pop concerts on Saturday nights. I've got them in there.'

'Do they have to wear roller skates?'

'Don't take the piss, Timmo. You're a nice boy but you've got to learn to be serious sometimes. This pop game is not for mugs, you know. Tomorrow night. I got them in at short notice because some other group dropped out with Dutch Elm Disease.'

'That's great, Sid. What do they sound like?'

Sid looks sheepish. 'Well, they all sound the same, don't they?'

'I wouldn't have said that, Sid. What are they, hard-rock?'

Sid begins to look shiftier than a ton of eels. 'Well, to tell you the truth, I haven't heard them.'

'You what!!??'

'No it was funny. You know I said they were playing above this pub? Well, I bumped in to Fred Nunger. You remember Fred?' I find it easy to shake my head from side to side. 'No? Well, he was in the public and we had a few drinks. Lovely fellow, Fred. Great sense of humour. I'm certain you must have met him. Tall bloke with—'

'How did you manage to miss the group, Sid?'

'By the time I got upstairs they'd finished. Of course, I did hear a bit. Every time I went to the karsi I could hear them bashing away!'

'So, because of what you heard while you were having a piss you were prepared to lash out a hundred quid a week? You must have had a skinful.'

'Fred liked them.'

Blimey! Sid is like a big soft kid, isn't he? Rosie still buys his pants for him.

'Did Fred hear them?'

'No, but he saw them. We both saw them.' Sid tries to sound convincing. 'They were very impressive. You know how important appearances are in this game?'

There are a lot of things I feel like saying, but – what is the point? If you get lumbered with Sid you have to put up with this kind of caper. If I wanted to make money I would go down and chuck myself through the window of the labour exchange.

Sid always operates on the principle that attack is the best form of defence – it is about the only principle he has – and is swift to fill the silence left by my disgust.

'It's no good standing there with a face as long as a Hashamite's hampton,' he snaps. 'There's work to do. I can't carry the whole show. You've got to get out there and earn your keep.'

'You mean, earn Kipper's keep,' I say.

'It comes to the same thing, Timmo. It's all an investment. You've got to show a lot more vision if you want to get on in life.'

Sometimes I feel I could really hang one on him but I manage to control myself. 'What do you want me to do, Sid?'

'I'm making you Public Relations Officer for the group. When they open at the Rollerdrome tomorrow night I want to see it splashed across every front page in the country.'

'Be reasonable, Sid.'

'Reasonable, smeasonable!!' Look out, Bernard Delfont, here comes Sid. 'You've got to use a little initiative if you want to make news. Get a load of scrubbers to storm the boys' dormobile – not before midday, they'll still be kipping – alert the local press. Get a human interest story with a local slant. One of the group must have been born near here: "I always knew I'd do it on my own doorstep" that kind of thing.'

'Sounds more like confessions of a secret sennapod sipper.'

Sid shakes his head sullenly. 'There you go again. You can't be serious, can you? Stop messing about and go and meet the boys. Once you've done that you'll have a better idea of what to do with them.'

'They don't really live in a dormobile, do they?'

Sid looks as if he does not care for the note of criticism in my voice. 'You expect me to put them up at the Ritz? Only a few minutes ago you were whining because I'd signed them up.'

'It's just that living in a dormobile doesn't make them sound very successful, Sid.'

'They're at the beginning of the great adventure, Timmo. They haven't tasted success yet. With your loving care and enthusiasm they can be turned into something fantastic. Now get out there and start moulding.'

'Get out where, Sid?'

'Oh.' Sid scratches his bonce. 'I think they're parked round the south side of the common, between the refreshment hut and the toilets.'

Sid is right. At least, I imagine he must be when I see the battered dormobile bouncing up and down beside the kerb. The sides are covered in scratches and biro messages saying things like 'I love you, Fuggy', 'Nutter is the greatest' and 'Wankers', crossed out. As I come round the side of the heaving heap I find a tall, spindly geezer painting 'Pete Williams is the best bass guitarist in the world' in a bit of spare space. It is reassuring to know that the group do have a few fans even if some of them are male.

I look at my watch. It is a quarter to twelve. The group should be ready to rise. I nod at the bloke with the paint brush and give a sharp rat-tat-tat on the door. It might have been a sharp tat-rat-rat, I can't really remember. After a couple of moments the dormobile stops shuddering and the door slides open.

'Morning,' I say, brightly. 'I'm Timmy Lea and—'

I don't get a chance to finish my sentence because a tall, hairy geezer pushes past me and starts having a slash against one of the wheels.

'Great, just great,' he says. I think he is referring to the piss. He is certainly not referring to the pong that leaks out of the dormobile. It is enough to make the wick on a bottle of air freshener shrivel up and die. There are now three blokes and two birds in the van and when I cop an eyeful of the judy dropping her dress over her nut I can see why the suspension was getting a work out. Thank goodness life has equipped me to deal with this kind of thing without showing too much of the embarrassment that naturally floods through me.

'Ta, ta, Nutter,' says the bird with the clothes on. 'I'd better be going otherwise I'll be late for school. I don't want to miss dinner, it's fish fingers today.'

'I'm Fuggy,' yawns the geezer in the string vest. 'Right, piss off. See you.'

Obviously not secretary of the Godfrey Winn Memorial Society, I think to myself. I will have to watch myself with these lads. It would be nasty if I became tainted.

Miss Gaol Bait scampers away and her kid sister begins to disentangle herself from the bald geezer who has two eyes painted on the top of his nut. This feature might cause a few cups to quiver in the Cheltenham Conservative Club but it is the bright green background that I find most disturbing. Where most people have hair, this geezer has menthol fresh flesh.

'I thought you was Fuggy,' says the bint scratching the inside of her leg – it is what she is scratching it with that makes me avert my eyes.

Grasshopper Nut removes her hand and runs one of his own through the fuzz on top of his bonce. 'I used to be, he says. 'But the vibrations were fouling up my mandolin strings.' He looks me up and down. 'What brings you here, Earth Man?'

'Sidney told me to pop round and see you,' I say, putting on my eager, 'nice doggy' voice.

'Can he contract the skin on the top of his head?'

'I don't think so,' I say.

Grasshopper Nut shakes his head slowly. 'I wouldn't want to know a man like that,' he says thoughtfully.

'Nutter really feels,' says a little fat bloke admiringly.

'I know what you mean,' I say. I do, too. So must the bird. Really! It is amazing what people get up to these days. They seem to have no shame, some of them. Nutter stops feeling, long enough to have another little scratch and the bloke who was having a leak comes in.

'I remember Sidney – ouch!' he says. He says 'ouch!' because he makes a pig's ear of stowing away his donger. 'Pissed out of his mind. Said he was going to put us on at the Albert Hall.'

'I must have been somewhere else at the time,' says Nutter.

'You always are,' says the tall hairy bloke. 'Why don't you give it up? Your eyes look like they just ran out of your hooter.'

'You're all lined up for the Rollerdrome, tonight, are you?' I say, trying to capture a note of brisk efficiency.

Four fifths of Kipper look at me blankly while the bird starts to pull on a pair of panties like we were not there.

'Oh yeah. Some gig he was rambling on about.' The bloke in the string vest starts to scratch himself for a change.

'Wish me luck for the netball,' trills the bird.

'We might be down later,' says Short Arse. 'Which convent are you at?'

'I've come to organise some publicity for the group,' I chirp. 'I don't suppose any of you are local lads?'

'I was nearly a local lag,' says Fuggy. 'I appeared at the South West London Magistrate's Court.'

'Breaking and entering the classics,' says Hairy.

'Watch it, Rat Knackers!'

'Cool it, you cats. If I don't have inner peace while I'm meditating it stunts my arpeggios.' Nutter lies back and closes his lower set of eyes. Something tells me that it is going to be difficult to get through to these boys.

'Would you like to tell me something about yourselves?' I say.

Hairy looks at me suspiciously. 'You haven't come to repossess the dormobile, have you?'

'Nothing like that,' I say evenly. 'Like I said, I'm here on behalf of Noggo Enterprises. I want to get a few background details so I can use them to publicise your concert tonight. Sid – Mr Noggett did give you some money, didn't he?'

The group look at Hairy with sudden interest.

'After I'd refused five hundred "Hulapog" sets,' he says grudgingly. 'I mean, I don't want to chuck a pogo stick through a hula hoop.'

'Neither does anyone else,' I say soothingly. 'Right. So you have a contractual obligation?'

'We call them withdrawal symptoms in the trade,' says Fuggy.

'He doesn't mean that, you stupid berk,' snaps Hairy. 'Talk to me, Mr Leak. I'm the brains of this outfit.'

'Where's the bread, Trembler?' says Short Arse.

'I'm withholding it for expenses,' says Hairy. 'If I started dishing it out now there'd be nothing left.'

'But there never is anything left.'

Trembler clearly decides that he can go through life ignoring remarks like that and turns to me. 'Let me give you a run down on the group,' he says. 'Nutter is what we call a "head" pianist. You know how some people play by ear? Well, Nutter bashes his whole bonce against the keys.'

'That's why I keep it very smooth,' murmurs the great man. 'I marry my mind to my music.'

'Why green?' I ask.

'It's my favourite colour. Have you ever rested a cabbage on a keyboard? It's poetry, man.'

'Nutter used to be with "A and O" then he left to form his own group "Suckling Pip". When that broke up he went to "Knockers Yard". Then came six months inside.'

'That's another group, is it?' I ask.

'No. It was for shop lifting.'

'Like I was just feeding myself, man,' says Nutter. 'The artist has to survive. I can look after the inner man but the outer man needs sustenance. Know what I mean?'

'Fuggy plays drums and he used to be with London Transport.'

'On the buses?' I ask.

'No. The group. This little chap—' Hairy indicates Short Arse. 'Labours under the monnicker of Reg Sharp. He is only interested in gelt and plays a bad bass guitar.'

'Trembler, don't be like that. I was only—'

'Shut your trap, Creeper! I've finished talking about you. Pete Williams plays bass guitar and dreams about having it off with a Moog Synthesiser.'

'What's that?'

Trembler shakes his head. 'You don't get around much, do you? It's a box of wires like a telephone switchboard that makes more noises than a tart on a sex maniacs' outing.'

'Where is Pete Williams?' I ask.

'Right behind you.'

I turn round and there is the bloke who was painting 'Pete Williams is the best bass guitarist in the world' on the side of the dormobile.

'How do,' he says. 'I ran out of paint.'

'You can borrow some of Nutter's,' says Fuggy.
'I don't fancy green,' says Pete.
'What do you do?' I ask Trembler.
'I dance around a bit. Bash my tambourine. Drive the chicks out of their minds. I'm just a love object, really.'
'And how long have you been together?'
'As a group, you mean?' Trembler thinks hard. 'About two and a half weeks.' My heart plunges past my goolies. 'How many engagements have you had in that time?'
'Just the one.'
'At the pub?'
'That's right. It was a bit of a dead loss, though.' Everybody in the dormobile starts nodding.
'What happened?' I say, wishing I did not have to ask.
'None of our plugs fitted their sockets so they had to play records.'
'So you mean you haven't actually played together?'
'Not in front of an audience. But we've had a few sessions, haven't we, lads?'
'We'll be all right on the night,' says Fuggy.
'If I can barrow a guitar,' says Short Arse.
'You haven't lost it again! ?' says Trembler. 'It's getting past a joke.'
'I must have left it in the gents,' says Short Arse. 'You know when we were busking in the underpass—'
'That was bloody stupid too,' scolds Trembler. 'You must have known I didn't mean the one with cars going through it.'
I tune out their voices and consider the desperate gravity of the situation Sid has dropped us in. He must have been listening to records every time he went out to the karsi. Only Sidney Noggett could sign up a group that had never played a note together for a hundred quid a week. No wonder they jumped at it. Oh my gawd!
'I think I've got enough to be going on with,' I say truthfully. 'You haven't got a fan club or anything like that? I want to organise a little demonstration around your appearance tonight.'

'Nothing special,' says Trembler. 'Women just respond naturally to our animal magnetism.'

I notice that everyone in the dormobile is now scratching – including me. It is probably time I moved on.

'I'll see you later,' I say. 'Good luck with the show.'

'So long, squire. Give our regards to Mr Noggett.'

Outside the dormobile, Pete Williams is now at work with a nail file: 'Pete Williams has a big fu'!

'How do you spell "future"?' he asks.

I walk away feeling decidedly uneasy. Noggo Enterprises is definitely in stuck. I am not one to point the finger at anybody but in the whole of my natural I have never seen a more repulsive load of layabouts. Dirty, smelly and – 'Cop that, you sod!' I hardly have time to look up before a middle-aged geezer I have never seen before tries to change the shape of my jaw with a bunch of fives. I sit down in the gutter with time to think about things.

'You touch my daughter again and I'll smash your ugly face in!'

Behind me I hear the sound of a dormobile being forced into gear.

'You made a mistake, mate,' I say. 'I'm not part of Kipper.'

'You won't be part of a fish finger if I catch you sniffing round my Myrtle again,' says the bloke.

The dormobile is now pulling away from the kerb – fast.

'Is that one of them?' Another geezer is approaching fast. He is bigger and uglier than the first one and is dragging a sobbing bird by the arm. Her face is only slightly well less known to me than some of her other features.

'I don't know, Dad.'

'I'm going to kill him!!'

Right! That's it. Goodbye everybody. I scramble to my feet and start legging it across the common. Ahead of me I can see the dormobile waiting to push out into the traffic by Clapham South Tube Station. It pauses for a minute and then disappears behind a 189 bus.

CHAPTER FOUR

In which Kipper makes a memorable debut at the Rollerdrome and Timmy receives succour at the hands – and other things – of Belinda Muckredge, enthusiastic cub reporter.

I am not over flattered when I consider that the two geezers who were trying to punch lumps out of me thought I looked like one of the Kipper mob. I had always fancied myself as being a bit on the clean-cut side. I worry about it all the way to the offices of the *South London Sentinel.* Where to start rustling up press coverage had also been a problem. How can you call a group local when they live out of a dormobile and never sleep in the same place twice? In the end I decide that we might as well use *my* local newspaper. Taking a last look over my shoulder I bound up the narrow flight of stairs.

At the top is a desk and behind it a bored chick filing her nails. If the sight of me makes her want to rip open the front of her dress and expose the ripe fruit of her breasts she thinks better of it by the time she has finished parking her gum.

'Yes?' she says.

'I've got an exciting event I'd like to discuss with someone,' I say.

'Triplets?' she says. 'I'm sorry. We've had this week's quota.' I don't know what she is on about but I press on regardless.

'No, it's this fantastic local group. They're having a big opening.'

'You mean, the Womens' Institute Jumble Sale?'

If I was Humphrey Bogart I would slap her round the chops a couple of times. I mean, some people are so out of touch, aren't they? I should have taken the story to *The Sun.*

'I'd like to talk to someone,' I say patiently.

'You'd better go through to Mr Muckredge,' she says.

'What is he?' I say, allowing an edge of exasperation to creep into my voice. 'Editor? Features? Advertising?'

'Yes,' she says. 'Third door on the right.'

When I get into the office, the big desk seems to be completely covered with piles of papers and tabby cats. The old geezer behind the desk looks me up and down over the top of his specs and nods towards one of the piles.

'Deaths? Over there, please.'

'I've got a big news story,' I say. 'A fantastic new pop group called Kipper are opening tonight. They're all local boys and there's going to be a lot of excitement. It would make a great front page story.'

Mr Muckredge shakes his head. 'I can't do that. We've already got the old age pensioner who was bitten by a fox.' Mr M. leans forward challengingly. 'At the top of a block of high rise flats! She heard something at the door, opened it, and the fox ran in and bit her.'

'It must have been a dog,' I say. 'You wouldn't get a fox up there. I mean, it wasn't being chased by a pack of hounds, was it?'

Mr M.'s face clouds over for a second. 'I didn't check that. No, I don't think it could have been. Otherwise, people would have seen them. Especially if they had all the horses and the pink jackets. People notice things like that on the Clem Attlee estate.'

I nod my head in agreement.

'Anyway, Mrs Tincy identified the animal.'

'You caught it, did you?' I say eagerly.

'No. We showed her a photograph of a fox. I've got it here somewhere. Yes, here we are.'

Mr Muckredge hands me a photograph of a woman holding a large marrow.

'She recognised it from this, did she?' I say patiently.

'She was positive.'

'That's amazing, isn't it?'

Notice the subtle way I am changing my tactics. If the foot in the door doesn't work, try squeezing a little soft soap through the keyhole. I haven't had all my selling experience for nothing, you know – dance like a butterfly, sting like a bee, you can stuff your insects, there's no flies on me.

'You've got a photograph, of course?' inquires Mr M.

'Nothing has happened yet,' I say, getting worried. 'I thought you would take the photographs.'

Mr Muckredge shakes his head as if surprised that people as simple as myself were allowed to walk the streets without the company of someone in a white coat.

'That can be very expensive,' he says. 'And there is no guarantee of getting the best results. Most people who give us a story provide their own photograph. Of course, this fox—' Mr M. holds up a photo of two babies – 'was different. Mrs Cartright didn't have a camera with her when she opened the window.'

'Uuuuum. I see,' I say. 'So it would be better if I took the photographs and wrote the story?'

Mr M. nods unenthusiastically. 'I try and use everything I get, but as you can see, there's an awful lot to get through. I'm five weeks behind with the cinema ads.'

Better men than me – there must be some, somewhere – might decide at this minute to jack the whole thing in and take up pot-holing, or hop-poling, or anything but, suddenly, as is its wont, something happens. A door flies open and a beautiful, blonde-haired dumpling factory flows into the room. She has more soft edges than a dollop of cream and her legs must be chafing the undersides of her armpits.

'I'm sorry to come barging in, Nunky,' she says. 'But I've got the printers on the phone. They seem rather excited.'

Muckredge shoots a glance at me and rubs his hand over his mush.

'I'll take it in your office,' he says to the bird and scuttles out. Blondy turns on a smile like the bars of an electric fire and starts stroking one of the cats. The way she does it makes percy shiver.

'I hope I'm not interrupting something important?' she says.

'I'm afraid you aren't,' I say. 'I was trying to get Mr Muckredge to do a feature on this new pop group, but I don't think he has got the space.' I am not telling her all this because I think I have a future reading children's fairy stories on the tele but because something deep inside tells me that she may be able to help me. The expression on her mug suggests that I may be right.

'Oh, dear, What a shame.' She sighs. 'I'm afraid Uncle Phil is a bit of an old stick in the mud. If you haven't got a big cucumber there's not much chance of getting on the front page.'

'Really,' I say.

A bright new light dawns across the bint's face. 'I wonder if he'd let me handle it,' she says thoughtfully.

I try not to think about the implications of the nice blonde handling my cucumber and allow my mince pies to widen in healthy eagerness.

'That would be smashing,' I say. 'The group is called Kipper and I'm certain they're going to make a big impression.'

'Of course, I'm only the cub reporter,' says the bird. 'But then, that's all I've ever done: cubs, brownies and flower shows. Come to think of it, I'm the *only* reporter. I'd forgotten that Mr Dalloway had retired.'

'I'd be very grateful,' I say, flaring my nostrils and ripping open a paper clip with my bare hands to show her the kind of stuff I'm made of. 'I was hoping we might get a few photographs.'

'We've got a camera.' The bird sounds so keen. 'I've never used it but I expect it's quite simple.'

She points to something that looks like the product of a shotgun marriage between an antique accordion and a gas mask. From the amount of dust on it, it seems unlikely that anyone else has used it.

'Uncle Phil is practically running the whole show by himself,' breaths my new help-mate. 'It's too much for him at his age.'

A strangled scream from the next office suggests that the strain may finally have told. We race to the partition in time to see the receiver crunch down onto the rest like a steam hammer.

'Bloody fools!' shouts an enraged Mr Muckredge. 'Why the devil should I pay their bills when they ruin my best story for weeks?'

'What happened, Uncle Phil?' says the bird.

Muckredge runs his fingers through his fast thinning hair.

'The headline I sent them was "Fox savages old age pensioner". Because I used an abbreviation for old age pensioner the stupid morons thought I'd left a letter out. The headline they've printed is "Fox savages soap."!!'

Mr Muckredge is so worked up that he agrees to everything Bindy says to him – yes, that is her name, Belinda Philips – and it is arranged that I will meet the bird outside the Rollerdrome at half past six in order to cover the group's arrival, the scenes of them being mobbed by thousands of fans, and dressing room interviews.

I would like to get closer acquainted with the enthusiastic Miss Philips but this will clearly have to wait. I have yet to mobilise the thousands of Kipper fans who, at this moment, do not even know that they exist. My first impulse is to nobble a few school kids but – blimey! You would not coco how suspicious people are these days. One teacher tries to bend an umbrella over my bonce and another disappears to call the fuzz. I was only passing sweets through the playground railings, too. If this kind of treatment goes on I will begin to get worried about myself.

Could it be that I actually look less than a thousand percent wholesome? In the end I round up about a dozen relatives, once removed – well, to be honest, most of them have been removed more than once – and limp back to Scraggs Lane feeling knackered. Nobody could fault my day for effort yet somehow I do not feel totally relaxed about the coming evening. Something deep inside me suggests that Noggo Enterprises may be on the brink of a diabolical cock up.

My mood is not improved by bumping into Dad on the front doorstep of the ancestral pile – or haemorrhoid as Mum would prefer to have it known. He is carrying a dozen umbrellas and it is clear that these represent the spoils of yet another hard day's work at the Lost Property Office.

'Expecting rain, are you, Dad?' I say cheerfully. It is in my nature, you see? I can't help trying to look on the bright side. I mean, you've got to these days, haven't you?

'Belt up, you sponging little git!' Dad shoulders me out of the way and stamps into the house. I can sense that he is not in one of his better moods. 'Treat the bleeding place like a hotel, don't you?' I am practically mouthing the words along with him. 'The only time we see you is when you want feeding or you want to change your clothes.'

'I've been doing some work for Sid,' I say, stepping over the umbrellas – yesterday's umbrellas, that is.

'Work!' Dad spits out the word. Very unpleasant it is too. Luckily it hits one of the umbrellas and does not go on the carpet. 'You don't know the meaning of the word.'

'I should do, Dad. The number of times you've explained it to me.'

Dad wags a finger under my nose. 'Always trying to be smart, that's your trouble. You want to be a bit less smart and a lot more hard-working.'

Fortunately Mum appears wiping her flour-covered hands on one of Dad's vests. She is hopeless without her glasses.

'You should have told us where you were, dear. You might have been knocked down or something.'

'Yeah,' says Dad, thoughtfully.

'I'm sorry, Mum. I stayed the night with Sid and Rosie. It'll be nice their place, when they've furnished it.'

Mum shakes her head. 'That's all they're going to have, dear. Rosie has some funny ideas. I don't know where she gets it from.'

'No, Mum.' I look carefully at Mum and try and imagine her being whipped away by the Duke of Bedsox outside the stage door of the Imperial, Clapham Junction. I don't see it somehow.

'Is the grub up, yet?' says Dad. 'I'm starving.' He belches loudly to prove it. How nice it is to be back at the temple of gracious living. Half an hour later I escape trying to purge my mind of the memory of Mum's toad-in-the-hole – my stomach was purged thirty seconds after the first mouthful. For the life of me I would swear that she uses real toads. Honestly, if I was not a creature of habit I would never go within twenty miles of Scraggs Lane without a stomach pump.

I struggle across London to the Rollerdrome. When Bindy rolls up in a Mini I think what a berk I was not to have hitched a lift from her. What a knockout bird she is. Amidst these drab, grey streets she looks like a rose petal that has drifted on to a cow pat.

'Not many people here,' she says.

The same thought has been occurring to me. Not one of my mob has turned up and the street is emptier than the centre of Glasgow on a flag day. The hall itself looks like a doss house and the stained glass windows hardly help to make the building throb with vitality. The best thing about the scenery is the front of Bindy's jumper. It has a large sign on it saying "PRESS". I am tempted but I have too much on my mind.

'They don't seem to be on the programme,' says Bindy.

She is studying a poster outside the hall and I quickly inform her that Kipper are stepping in at the last moment – right in, it seems to me. I am beginning to get really worried when a gaggle of senior citizens wheezes round the corner. I don't take much notice until one of them comes up to me.

'Timothy Lea? I thought it was you dear. I'm Mrs Peters. Sonia's mother. She said you had some tickets for a free show. She couldn't come herself so I brought Mrs Dixon. You remember Rachel's mother? And Mrs Forcett. And Gran—'

She rambles on and I realise that I have got lumbered with a load of German fast bowlers – you know, geriatrics. Blimey, what a carve-up! How am I going to get this lot to mob Kipper? They would be pushed to help a wheel chair over the kerb.

'Hello, Mrs Peters,' I say, amazed by the warmth that flows from my lips. 'I hope it's going to be your cup of tea.'

'It's free, that's the main thing,' says Mrs P. giving my arm a squeeze.

'Well, yes, sort of.' I take a quick shufti at the assembled bints and come to a conclusion – you know what I mean, nothing dirty intended. They are not going to turn a scotsman's kilt into a flareline but they are better than nothing. 'Excuse me, ladies. Before you go in there's something I'd like you to do for me?'

Half an hour later it has started to rain and Kipper have still not turned up. The senior citizens hover in the foyer and look at me suspiciously. Bindy is getting worried and I am petrified. I knew this would happen – or rather, not happen. The filthy finks will fail to show up and Noggo will be in dead stuck.

'Any minute now, ladies,' I say cheerfully. You can tell I was a Holiday Host at Melody Bay Holiday Camp, can't you? We had a bloke there who could announce an outbreak of cholera in the canteen so you fell about laughing.

'What's happening? Where are they?' Sid has materialised like a pee stain on your new denims.

'We're still waiting for them, Sid.'

'We?' Sid takes in the crowd in the foyer – he has taken

in a lot of people in his time. 'I thought they were sheltering from the rain. Where are the fans?'

'They *are* the fans,' I whisper out of the corner of my mouth. 'And some of them are getting a bit unhappy about it. Don't talk too loud. The bird with the big knockers is press coverage.'

'That's all we've got, is it?' says Sid.

'I would be very happy with that,' I say.

Sid takes a longer look. 'I see what you mean,' he says.

Further chat is denied us because a familiar dormobile lurches round the corner.

'O.K. ladies, Bindy, let's have you!' I shout.

The dormobile scrapes along the kerb and Mrs Peters and friends prepare to brave the elements.

'Don't put your umbrellas up – oh, Gordon Bennet!' says Sid.

Like a flock of knock-kneed carrion crows the mothers of South West London stumble towards the dormobile.

'Ready, Bindy!' I shout. It may not be much but at least it is going to be captured for posterity. Bindy levels her apparatus and – hey! Mrs Dixon has just got abreast of the driver's window – and what a breast it is, too – when the dormobile starts to pull away. Maybe the scene reminds the boys of this morning on Clapham Common. It probably happens all the time. The back door flies open and three naked birds flop out into the gutter. They scramble up and run after the van.

'Come back!' I yell.

One of the birds turns round and starts running towards me.

'Not you. The van.'

'Oh dear.' Bindy is staring at her camera. 'I don't think anything happened.'

Sid gives an ugly choking laugh. 'It doesn't matter, darling. We don't really need a picture of a load of old faggots with umbrellas chasing a dormobile.'

'Thanks a lot, ladies,' I say pleasantly. 'Enjoy the show.'

'We can go in now, can we?' says Mrs Peters. She sounds puzzled. You can't blame her, really, can you?

'I think I'll throw myself under the next lorry,' says Sid. 'Blimey, but you don't half know how to cock things up, don't you?'

'Don't give me that, Sid,' I snarl. 'At least I wouldn't sign up a load of blokes who had never played a note of music together in their lives.'

'What's the matter?' says Bindy. 'Where have they gone?'

Sid gets himself under control with difficulty. 'I don't know,' he says. 'We'll have to go round to the dressing rooms and wait.'

The dressings rooms are another surprise. I mean, there aren't any. Or rather, we aren't allowed in them.

'No, no,' says an ancient geezer with a mug like an albino prune. 'If it wasn't made clear to you it should have been. We've had too much trouble in the dressing rooms. All performers have to make their own arrangements.' No sooner has he spoken than Trembler creeps round the corner.

'Have they gone?' he says. 'They're the worst, you know. What they can get up to with those umbrellas makes the Chinese water torture seem like a Soho massage parlour.'

'You'll have to change in the nearest gents,' says Sid. Sid does not mess about with small talk.

'I don't reckon that,' says Trembler. 'You don't know what it's like with all those instruments. The last time we had to do it, Fuggy turned round and knocked out Nutter with his guitar. Luckily there was some water handy—'

'Yes, yes,' interrupted Sid. 'Don't make a Royal Command out of it. Get your clobber on and get back here. You're on in five minutes.'

'What about the dressing room interviews?' said Bindy. 'I'm itching for a bit of action.'

'Then hang about, girl,' says the hairy leader of Kipper,

menacingly. 'They don't call me Trembler for nothing. Whooo Hoooo!'

'Get out of it, you daft sod,' snaps Sid. 'There's plenty of time for that when I've had a bit. Remember, this is your big gig. Make the most of it.' Trembler says something I would never even have thought about in front of a lady and pisses off.

'Nerves,' explains Sid. 'He's highly strung, like an electric cable. All great artists are the same. Let's go and have a look at the audience.'

I had not been looking forward to this moment, fearing that Mrs Peters and friends might be sitting on their tods but, to my relief, the hall is half full and people are still coming in. Most of them have probably come to see 'Goose Juice' who are topping the bill but that does not matter too much. What we need at the moment is an audience – any audience. We peer through a gap in the curtain and watch Mrs Peters and Co. huddling together like the tide is coming in on their seats.

'I can't see them storming the stage, can you?' says Sid.

'Only to get their bus fares back,' I tell him.

An occasion like this makes me realise how few real friends I have got. Ask people to do you a little favour and what happens? You don't see them for dust. The last couple of days have been very sobering ones. I will have to take serious stock of myself, once I find out what it means.

'Blimey!' says Sid. 'Look who's in the third row.'

'Who.'

'Gerry Valium!'

'Not "The Pundit Of Pop"?' I say. 'Not "The Prince Of Denmark Street"?'

'Yes, yes,' breathes Sid. 'A word from him can make us. Fancy him coming out here.'

'It's not surprising, Sid,' I say. 'He combs every corner of our septic isle for "now news of past-blasting outta-future groups". That's what keeps him a jump ahead. You're sure it's him?'

'Positive. I'd recognise those six inch high shades anywhere. He was the mystery object on "Stifle The Badger".'

'Of course he was!' I haven't seen Sid so excited since Uncle Ron made a mistake and laced a blue film into the 16mm epic of the family holiday at Broadstairs. Aunty Flo had just started sucking a lolly when, suddenly, there we were on this settee. Well, it gave me a shock, I can tell you. Aunty Flo had hysterics and Uncle Ron knocked over a bottle of Sanatogen. It was the last Boxing Day we ever spent with them.

'He has a column in the *Guardian*,' says Sid. 'Nobody ever reads it but they reprint it in *Melody Maker* as an ad.'

'You don't really need me any more, do you?' says Bindy sadly.

'Course we do,' I say. 'We still haven't got those dressing room interviews.' I give her hand a little squeeze. 'Come and sit in the audience. You'll get a better feel of things there.'

'If you sit next to him you will,' says Sid coarsely. 'You two go on ahead. I want to give the boys a pep talk.'

I steer Bindy away from Mrs Peters and her crowd and find a couple of seats behind Gerry Valium. The hall is quite full now.

'It's exciting, isn't it?' says Bindy.

I nod.

'Are you nervous?'

I nod again. I am not so much nervous as in danger of warping the woodwork. I have less faith in Kipper than in a plastic charm bracelet. If the five of them can appear on stage without falling over each other I will be amazed. If they actually appear at all I will be losing money to myself. Trembler probably looked in to see if he could nick someone's wallet.

'Ladies and gentlemen, as the first space men land in Finsbury Park we bring you . . . . . .' The voice comes over the loudspeaker system as Sid appears from the door beside the stage. He is not exactly wringing his hands but it is clear that he is in a state bordering on the distressed.

'Oh my Gawd!' he says.

'Sit down, Grandad,' says a spotty herbert sitting behind us.

'What's the matter, Sid?' I ask.

'One of the bleeders hasn't got an instrument. They said you knew about it?'

'I thought he'd left it somewhere and was going to pick it up.'

'Well, someone else picked it up first.'

'What's happened? Has he stood down?'

Sid snarls, 'I wish he'd stand down a manhole. No, he refuses to be left out. He says he's going on.'

'. . . Kipper!' Before Sid can give news of further disasters, the curtain goes up.

I make a quick count of the geezers on the stage and – blimey! They are all there. Short Arse is trying to wrestle a guitar from Pete Williams but a quick bash over the nut from Trembler quietens him down. He stands still for a moment and then starts to play an imaginary instrument. Sid buries his face in his hands.

Trembler has his own problems. A touch of the Jason Noggetts has affected his satin knee breeches and a glance at the group is enough to suggest that they could all have done with more time in the dressing room. Most of them clearly have problems playing their instruments with two hands. To play with one hand while the other holds up their trousers is beyond them.

'Are they going to do striptease?' whispers Bindy.

I do not answer her because my attention is focussed on Nutter. As the curtain went up, he was trying desperately to prise open the lid of the piano. With a fresh shudder of horror – how many shudders of horror before my circuit becomes over-loaded? – I realise that the management must have forbidden use of the hall's instruments as well as its dressing rooms. The piano is locked.

Nutter battles on bravely and then, suddenly, bashes his

bonce against the piano lid. There is a cheer from the audience. Nutter bashes again. A louder cheer.

The rest of the group have scraped together some kind of noise and against this, Nutter rises to his feet and brings his nut down, like a bird pecking. The piano lid splinters and Nutter rips it aside with his bare hands. Now that the keys are exposed he runs his green bonce along them and the audience go mad. A couple of good bashes and the whole contraption starts to wobble. I can see the manager running down the aisle while Gerry Valium starts forward in his seat. Sid is groaning.

Nutter drops to his hands and knees and charges the piano. The audience are on their feet, my feet – anybody's feet. Short Arse steps forward to one of a battery of microphones and starts playing his invisible instrument like his fingers are going to drop off. Even if he had a guitar I wouldn't be able to hear it above the noise the audience are making.

'Concert grand!' screams the manager.

'Oh no!' groans Sid.

Nutter bashes his bonce against one of the piano legs and the structure tilts. Another crunch and there is a noise just like a grand piano collapsing. Nutter dives on top of it and starts – well, I don't really like saying what he starts doing. Maybe his flies get snagged up in the working parts.

The manager leaps up on the stage and starts waving his arms and the curtain comes down.

'They're different aren't they?' says Bindy.

'They're going to be different,' snarls Sid. 'Their own mothers won't recognise them when I've finished with them.'

In front of us Gerry Valium leaps to his feet and strides purposefully towards one of the exits.

'See what you've done?' hisses Sid. 'There goes our big break. I give you a chance to prove yourself and you blow it. Well, that's it. I'm washing my hands of you. You can pay for that piano out of your own pocket money.' Before

I can say anything – like 'piss off, cony-cobblers' – Sid has stalked off in a high dudgeon. I would prefer to see him in a low dungeon, myself, but I can wait.

'Oh dear,' says Bindy. 'He isn't very pleased, is he?'

It is difficult to disagree with her. 'He's invested a lot of money in the group,' I say.

'The audience seemed to like them,' says Bindy.

The bloke behind me is stabbing his seat with a flick knife and all over the hall similar acts of spontaneous joy are breaking out. A geezer tries to nut open an exit door which turns out to have been padlocked while the stewards struggle with another group who are practising on each other. Birds are screaming and in the distance I hear the familiar wail of an ambulance siren.

'I don't think there's much point in us hanging around here,' I say.

'What about the interviews?'

'In the circumstances—' I stretch out an arm and nonchalantly catch a bottle as it whizzes past '—I think we might give them a miss.'

The near psychic qualities that I possess when it comes to analysing the behavioural patterns of birds suggest to me that Bindy is not exactly chuffed to bollocks with her part in the evening so far. As to my part – well, that is what I am going to start thinking about. You can spend just so much time pouring out your life to other people.

'Don't go that way,' I say.

At the end of the row, Mrs Peters has battered her umbrella into a semi-circle and another rocker sinks to his knees. I suppose it makes a change from lantern slides at the Women's Institute.

Bindy changes direction and we scamper up the aisle and out into the North London night.

'What are we going to do now,' says Bindy.

'I wouldn't mind having a look at what you've got in there.' I am of course referring to the camera slung round her neck but it is amazing how birds jump to the wrong conclusions, these days.

'I hardly know you,' she says, making a token attempt at pulling her jacket over her titties.

I attempt a blush and rephrase my statement.

'I have a small dark room at my place,' she says. 'We could go there if you like.'

'That would be smashing,' I say. 'You're sure it's not going to be any trouble?'

She looks me up and down. 'I don't know. It might be.'

I am expecting her to be living with Mum and Dad, or Nunky, and it is a pleasant surprise to find that she has a flat in one of the posh developments off Wandsworth Common. It is so smooth that the lifts are working and the dustbins have lids on them.

'I can do you some beans on toast while we're waiting,' she says. 'Fix yourself a drink while I freshen up. There's some beer in the fridge.'

I must say, I am getting off with a better class of bird these days. It probably has something to do with all the B.B.C. 2 I have been watching. Women are quick to respond to a man who can tell them the semi-finalists in the Rugby League Floodlit Trophy Competition. I help myself to a lager and go into the living room.

'I won't be a minute,' sings out Bindy.

The door to her bedroom is not quite closed and thanks to the handy positioning of a mirror on the living room wall I get a Peeping Tom's view of my hostess in panties and bra. Of course, nobody with any pretensions to being a gentleman would take advantage of such an opportunity so I drink in the scene eagerly. When she starts scratching her thatching I jerk half my lager across the carpet – it's a good way of making your drink go further.

'Did you have an accident?' she says when she comes into the room and finds me on my hands and knees. 'I see you found a dish cloth.'

It is my handkerchief, actually, but I decide that it is

probably better not to say anything.

'Nearly finished,' I say in my best Mrs Mop manner. 'That's a smashing dress you're wearing.'

It is, too. It has a big slit down the side and dragons all over it. For two pins it could have me all over it, and all.

'I got it in Hong Kong,' she says. 'It's ideal for lounging about in. I like loose clothes, don't you?'

'Yes,' I say – I am very quick like that. 'Do you have this place all to yourself?'

'No, I share it with another girl. She'll be back tomorrow.'

Nice of her to tell me that, I think to myself. Could it be that this buckshee info is intended to tip me the wink that a spot of unrefereed in and out is on the cards?

'Better get down to it,' says Miss P. as if she has been reading my mind. 'Do you know anything about photography?'

'I always take my snaps to Boots.' I say, watching the way her robe flops open as she fiddles with the back of her camera.

'I can't guarantee that anything is going to come out.'

'No.' I say thoughtfully. When I was younger I used to try and take advantage of remarks like that. But now I am older and more sophisticated I don't bother. You will notice that I have said nothing about going into a dark room and seeing what develops. Only time will tell if my suavity pays off.

'Can I do anything to help?' I say.

'Not really. It won't take a minute and then I'll get us a bite to eat while we're waiting.'

She trips off and I take a shufti into the bedroom. Two twin beds with a table between them. Her smalls are lying on the counterpane. See through jobs with little roses on them. Percy gives an eager flutter. Down boy! I will be nicking things off clothes lines if I'm not careful. Only the other week I found myself taking a long decco at the underwear counter in Marks and Sparks. Many of the great sex criminals have had humbler beginnings. After that it is but a short step to whipping open your plastic mac on the Circle Line and huddling up against the exit doors in the rush hour. I am suppressing a nervous shiver when a door opens and Bindy reappears.

'I'm afraid they were all exposed,' she says. 'There must have been something wrong with the camera. I am sorry. I've brought you round here for nothing.'

Don't speak too soon, I think to myself. Where there is a willy there is a way.

'It doesn't matter,' I say. 'After what happened tonight nobody is going to be interested in a photo of Kipper being eaten alive by dormice. They're finished before they've even begun.' I manage to sound broken up about it and Bindy is swift to respond.

'Poor Timmy. It hasn't been your day, has it?'

'Not one of the greatest,' I say, registering the sympathetic pressure of her hand on my arm.

'You will stay and have something to eat, won't you?'

'If it's not too much trouble.'

'No trouble at all. It'll only take a jiffy.'

She skips off to the kitchen and starts playing with the nobs on her cooker. Within seconds delicious whiffs of bacon are wafting up my hooter.

'Would you like to open some wine?'

It's too much, isn't it? We only need a couple of candles and it's going to look like the cover of *Ideal Home* Magazine.

'I'm starving,' I say. 'I haven't eaten all day.' It is quite true because I never count Mum's stuff as food.

The meal is really knock out and after it my stomach feels the same way about Miss Philips as the rest of me: we like her.

'That was the best thing I've had inside me for a long time,' I say.

Bindy raises an eyebrow. 'I think it would be immodest of me to say the same. Untruthful too.' She leans across the table and prods me with one of her long fingers. 'Are you feeling better now?'

'Much.' Like I have said before, birds who touch you are always good news. This one tucks into her nosh, as well, which is something I like. I feel uneasy when a bird cooks a smashing meal and then settles down opposite you with half a ryvita in her mit.

'I could fall asleep where I'm sitting.'

'Don't do that.' With the lean muscular grace of a young gazelle I rise to my feet and shoot half the things on the table onto the floor. I have tucked the table cloth into my trousers instead of the serviette. Oh dear. Why is it that Steve McQueen never does things like that?

'Monkeys!'

'I doesn't matter. It won't take a moment to clean up.'

The lovely Miss Philips disappears into the kitchen and within seconds is kneeling before me, her curvaceous knockers agitating to the movement of her dust pan and brush. The slit in her skirt reveals acres of tempting thigh and percy immediately starts to hoist himself into the present arms position. I reckon I would have been murder in one of those big Victorian houses with parlour maids scrambling about all over the place. You wouldn't know which way to turn, would you?

'Let me help you,' I say. I mean, help in the widest, truest sense of the word. I sink to my knees and 'OUCH!!'

In fact, that was not what I said but you have to be a bit careful these days. You are not allowed to print words like   and   . And even   is frowned upon in some circles. I understand that there are some printers who will not even touch   . Funny, isn't it?

Anyway, there I was, on my knees and suffering something awful, because I had knelt on a piece of broken glass.

'Oh no,' says Bindy. 'You poor thing. It's bleeding, isn't it?'

'Yes,' I say. 'I'm sorry about the rug.' It would have to be white.

'Don't worry about that. Get your trousers off and I'll do something.' Set that sentence to music and it would go to the top of every hit parade in the world.

'Are you sure?' I say, trying to remember when I last changed my Y-fronts.

'Don't worry. You can't shock me. I used to do the teas at K.C.S. Old Boys.'

I don't know what she is on about but I am not over-fussed. You don't stop to look at the number when you pick up a five pound note, do you?

'Come on the sofa, it'll be easier. Do you want any help?'

It is too much, isn't it? I allow the lady to peel off my trousers and try to keep a stiff upper lip. In fact, it is not the stiff upper lip I am most worried about. It is the stiff lower hampton. Sometimes I feel we are two separate people. There is the shy, sensitive Timothy Lea and the brash, thick-as-two-short-planks Pocket Python. It is like Jekyll and Heidi.

Just as I had feared, percy starts playing bell tents the minute my trousers have reached ankle level. Fortunately Miss P. is too much of a lady to make any comment. Either that or she is short sighted.

'There's nothing in there,' she says. It's just a cut. I'll put a dressing on it for you. Do you feel anything?'

'I do when you do that,' I say.

Bindy is running her hand over my knee like she is checking whether there is room to land a midget helicopter.

'You're ticklish, aren't you?' she says.

'It depends where you tickle me. Some parts are more sensitive than others.' Her mouth is very close to mine but I am not going to complain to the health authorities about it. I kiss her on the end of the nose and then steer a southerly course. By some strange accident of fate our lips find themselves having to push past each other to get anywhere.

'Hi,' says the lady.

'Hi.' It may not be dialogue that Shakespeare would

have woken his old lady up with, but it is good, tight pre lip-lumping stuff. Not in line for an academy award but excellent for the edge of a sofa in S.W.12.

'Can you move it?'

'No problem.'

We indulge in a little more mouth-melding and percy starts to act like one of those old roman catapults that used to throw Y-fronts over the castle walls at the enemy.

'The bleeding has stopped.'

'No dressing?'

'Not yet.'

This time, a hand brushes across Thomas the Tent Pole and Miss Philips sucks in her breath sharply.

'He's naughty, isn't he?' she says.

'Just friendly,' I murmur. 'He likes meeting people.'

'How do you do?' I suppose you could call what Bindy is doing shaking hands.

'Nicely, thank you,' I say, sending out my own digits on a fact-finding tour of the Hong Kong textile industry. 'What do you wear under this thing?'

'Keep going and you'll find out.'

I have never been slow to accept an invitation like that and soon my porky pandies are driving down the main street of Fursville. Conditions appear to be ideal for the big event and the whole community is throbbing with scarce suppressed excitement.

'I hope this is going to make up for the awful day you've had.'

Bindy peels off her panties and wades up my thighs for her appointment with percy.

'I'm sure it is,' I say. 'OoooooH! – I'm sure it is.'

CHAPTER FIVE

In which Kipper strike a hard bargain and Timmy is introduced to some of the sordid realities of the pop world – and has a nice time

'I hear it didn't go so well, last night,' chortles Dad. It is not often you see the old sod smile, I can tell you.

'Piss off!' snaps Sid.

'I'm not surprised, with a daft name like that,' continued Dad. 'Kipper. I ask you. I suppose they play sole music?'

Sid looks meaner than a ½p tip and Dad near pees himself. 'Did you hear that, mother? Sole music. I'll be the death of myself.'

'I wouldn't bet on it,' snarls Sid.

'We could always put them on at The Place,' I say, entering into the spirit of things.

'Belt up, Judas!'

'You've never haddock so good!' Dad is practically falling about. I have not seen him so happy since Aunty Edna pulled the chain and the cistern came down on her nut. Very nasty it was. I would not have been one of those ambulance men for all the tea in Typhoo. Sid buries his face in his cornflakes and silence rains – or reigns – or whatever you fancy. Anyway it is very quiet.

'Where's the paper?' says Dad.

'It's that new boy,' says Mum. 'He's left the *Guardian* again.'

'Gordon Bennett!' says Dad. 'Do I look as if I come from bleeding Manchester. I haven't got webbed feet, have I?'

'I don't know, Dad. You've never taken your socks off.'

'Watch it, sonny!' Dad does not mind dishing it out but he hates taking it.

'The *Guardian* is a very respected national organ,' says Sid in his 'Ascent of Man' voice.

'No need for that kind of talk, dear,' says Mum.

'If you like it so much, you have it,' says Dad. 'There's no pictures.' He chucks the paper at Sid and starts thumbing through the calendar we got from the off licence.

'Are you going to stay here permanently while you're doing this pop thing?' says Mum.

'Probably,' says Sid. 'Rosie is never at the house and I can't stand Gretchen's cooking. It's worse than – BLIMEY!' He has been thumbing through the paper and suddenly his head jerks forward as if it is on a piece of elastic.

'What's the matter, Sid.'

Sid shakes his head in disbelief. 'There's something here about Kipper.'

'Our Kipper?'

'I dunno.'

I race round to Sid's side of the table and take a shufti. Beneath a note saying that most of the reviews have appeared in late editions of the previous four days' *Guardians* is printed: 'Breakthrough.' I read on.

> 'Last night I was privileged to witness the single most important event in the history of music since the birth of Beethoven. At the Rollerdrome, Finsbury Park, Kipper gave us a new alphabet with which to write a new language. By breaking into a locked piano with his head, Nutter Normanton shattered our existing tenets of musical appreciation into a thousand fragments. He literally took his mind to the music and in so doing bypassed the agency of the intermediary tangible. He destroyed the complacency.
>
> In the same vein Reg Sharp played nothing beautifully and demonstrated that the instrument can in fact be a hindrance to the communication of a musical idea.
>
> That their participation in the concert broke up in

disorder is but a mark of Kipper's genius. It is difficult to recall, any first performance of outstanding brilliance that was not greeted with derision by morons.'

'What's he saying?' says Sid.

'I think he likes them,' I say.

'It's that bloke, isn't it? That Gerry Valium,' Sid is swelling before my eyes. 'Can I spot them? Can I not spot them? I told you those boys were magic.'

'Sid! You said they were a load of rubbish.'

'Nonsense! I never said that. You're putting words in my mouth.'

'Sid, be honest. You told me you went round to their dormobile and told them that the deal was off and that you were going to tear up the contract. Then they picked you up and threw you in the horse trough.'

Sid smiles sheepishly. 'Just horseplay. Neither of us meant anything by it. With kids like that you've got to lark around a bit.'

'*Did* you tear up the contract?'

Sid laughs like two pounds of giblets being fed into a vacuum cleaner.

'Do I look like some kind of idiot?' he says.

'Are you asking me?' says Dad.

'Belt up, rat-knackers,' snaps Sid. 'Of course, I didn't tear up the contract.' He walks to the door that gives onto the back yard and takes a deep breath. 'I won't be a minute.' He flashes out of the door like a scalded tom.

'What's come over him?' says Mum.

We peer out of the window and all that can be seen of Sid is his backside sticking out of one of the dustbins.

'I think's he misplaced something,' I say.

Fortunately the contract is found under a ton of tea leaves and Sid is practically crooning. In this mood he starts turning the same colour as a one pound note.

'Now all we've got to do is cut a disc and the moola will start rolling in,' he drools. 'I think I'll order the Citroen

Maserati now, I hear there's a long waiting list.'

'We've got to get signed up with a record company first, haven't we?' I say.

Sid is obviously saddened by my naivety. 'Record company – smeckord company!' he says. 'Why should we give our money away to Decca? Who needs them? Remember Bella? The Beatles have Apple. We have Bella. If you have your own label you get more gelt. It stands to reason. All we've got to do is milk this publicity and get a bit more. It shouldn't be difficult. The media will be fighting to get at them after this little lot.' He taps the paper.

'If they can find them.'

Sid starts to say something and then stops himself. A worried expression begins to spread across his mug. 'You don't reckon they'll be up the common?'

'Not after what happened yesterday. I nearly had to send my balls to the dry cleaners when those birds' dads caught up with me.'

'Rotten little sods!' Sid's face contorts in fury. 'I've got them under contract. They can't swindle me. I'll sue them for every penny they've got.'

'That should keep you in bubble gum for a couple of weeks,' I say. 'I reckon they're more skint than we are.'

'Life's full of problems, isn't it, dear?' says Mum philosophically. 'Why don't you have another cup of tea. That's what we used to do during the war.'

'Yes,' says Dad. 'While you were doing that, they dropped a bomb on the house next door, didn't they? Luckily Mrs Arbury had more sense than you. She was down the shelter.'

'It wasn't Mrs Arbury,' says Mum. 'Mrs Arbury ran off with the German prisoner of war she met on Wimbledon Common. I remember how upset her old man was when he came out of Stalagluft a hundred and eleven.'

'Stalagluft three, you stupid old moo,' says Dad. 'Blimey, don't you pay no attention to nothing? They have a film about it on the telly every other Sunday.'

A trip down memory lane is definitely on the cards and I follow Sid's example and slide towards the door.

'Right,' he says. 'We've got to find them. We're sitting on a potential gold mine.'

'That's what Dad used to say about Aunty Min,' I say. 'You'd never think, looking at her now, that she used to go out with all those Yanks during the war, would you?'

'Belt up about your bleeding Dad!' snarls Sid. 'This is serious. Have you got any idea where they might be?'

'From what I've seen of them I'd expect them to be somewhere near a pox doctor and an all-night chemist.'

My remark is not meant to be taken all that seriously but Sid looks thoughtful.

'St James's Park,' he says.

It seems as good a place to start as any but you could knock me down with a crow-bar when the first thing I see as we go through Admiralty Arch is a familiar, battered dormobile parked by the kerb. A clothes line has been tied to one of the flag posts and from it flutter five tea shirts with 'BLOATER' crossed out and 'KIPPER' substituted in biro – or rather, three 'KIPPER's one 'KIPER' and a 'KIPPA'.

'I think there's a bit of work to be done on the presentation side,' says Sid thoughtfully as we cross the road.

The Royal Standard is fluttering in the Mall – or it might have been the News, all I can remember is that it had 'Buck House' written in one corner – and I pocket it for Mum. She likes things like that. I expect that Phil chucked it out of the window of his carriage when he found that he did not have any winners up.

'Let me do the talking this time,' says Sid. 'The whole thing has got to be handled with a lot of finish and Jenny Quoits.' (Finesse and Je ne sais quoi? *Ed.*) I am prepared to take Sid's word for it and I step back respectively as the old master raps on the door.

'Piss off!' says a muffled voice.

'It's me, lads,' says Sid in his disgusting 'share my sweeties' voice. 'Sidney Noggett.'

'Piss off faster,' says the voice.

It takes another ten minutes of this kind of thing before a pong like the Festival Of Armpits announces that the door of the dormobile has slid open.

'You come for another batch?' yawns Trembler as he has his first public scratch of the morning – both public and private if you know what I mean.

'I've come to give you another chance,' says Sid. 'I think last night's disaster made us both act a little hastily.'

'But you tore up our contract?'

'That's right,' says Sid. 'But I didn't tear up *my* contract. We can pick up just where we left off.'

I think Trembler is looking round for a horse trough but I can't be certain.

'That's very big of you, Mr Noggett,' he says.

Sid prepares to switch on his 'Mr Wonderful, that's me' expression.

'The only trouble is—' Trembler produces a *Guardian* from behind his back '—we don't need you any more.'

Sid stops the door closing but it takes a few minutes to get the circulation moving through his fingers again.

'What are you on about?' he squeals. 'I gave you your first break. You can't do this to me. I made you. How did you get hold of that thing?' He jabs his finger at the *Guardian* like it came home on the bottom of somebody's shoe.

'We always read the papers before we turn in,' says Trembler.

'Now, piss off before I call the police.' He tries to shut the door again but Sid does not give up easily – not where money is concerned.

'Let's start from scratch,' he says. This is something that it is very easy to do with the inhabitants of the dormobile but before negotiations can be reopened – I got that phrase from the telly news – Fuggy appears carrying a pelican.

'Breakfast's up!' he says.

'Put it down, you daft sod!' says Trembler.

'It's all right. I'm doing it a favour putting it out of its misery. There's something wrong with the shape of its mouth. Somebody must have fed it half a brick.'

'Somebody ought to feed you half a brick,' says Trembler. 'Their mouths always sag like that. It's to store fish.'

'Maybe there's some fish in there.' Fuggy gets enthusiastic and tries to prise open the pelican's cakehole.

The pelican gives him a couple of minutes of its time and then pecks him in the balls. Fuggy screams and the pelican slowly flaps back towards the lake.

'I never knew they could laugh,' says Trembler.

'If there's something in the contract you're not happy about, I'm prepared to talk,' says Sid. It takes more than a pelican savaging someone's marriage prospects to divert Sid from the job in hand. Trembler is obviously a man after his own heart – and there aren't a lot of people after Sid's heart, I can tell you. Even Christian Barnyard didn't fancy it.

'All right, step inside and we'll have a natter,' he says.

'You two – out!' His last remark is addressed to a couple of ravers who look as if they might have outstayed their usefulness – they have their clothes on, anyway.

'Charming,' says the one with the candy-floss hair style – it is pink as well.

'I can see you never went to bleeding charm school.'

'Don't lower yourself, 'reen,' advises her less attractive friend. 'They're not worth it.'

'Get lost!' grunts Reg.

'You wait out here.' Sid addresses me as if I am a buff envelope. I am much less than loath to do so and as the door slides shut and the two birds ruffle their feathers I take a deep breath of smog and listen to the rippling note of a pigeon coughing. I used to be very keen on nature when I was a boy.

'What do you do?' says one of the birds.

'I'm an impresario,' I say.

'That's funny. They don't often admit it,' she says to her friend. They walk off towards Buckingham Palace while I look around for a brick. When Sid comes out his face is drawn. I would like to see the whole lot of him drawn – not to mention hung and quartered, but then, that is an acquired taste, I suppose. It comes from knowing the bastard.

Few words are spoken outside the dormobile and Sid drives away deep in silence.

'Sorted them out, did you?' I say brightly.

Sid accelerates towards an old age pensioner and shakes his head. 'I've had to change the deal a bit,' he says.

'Like how?' I ask.

'Like two hundred a week and a share of the profits.'

'What share?' I say.

'Wotcha,' says Sid.

'Don't mess about, Sid,' I say patiently. 'What share of the profits are we getting?'

'Twenty per cent.'

'Each?'

'Together.'

'Blimey, Sid. That's not very good, is it? I thought we were going to make a fortune out of these poor sods by exploiting them? At this rate they're exploiting us.'

Accepting criticism in the spirit in which it is offered has never been one of Sid's strong points and it is as well for the copper directing in Parliament Square that he has razor sharp reflexes.

'Shut your trap,' snaps my sensitive brother-in-law. 'I know what I'm doing. You have to judge every case on its merits. You've got to be flexible, like the government.'

'You'd make a wonderful Prime Minister, Sid.'

'Belt up, gopher-goolies! Can't you understand that

twenty per cent of a million quid is better than ninety per cent of a couple of hundred?'

'It's ending up with twenty per cent of a couple of hundred that's worrying me, Sid.'

'Think small. That's your motto, isn't it?' sneers Sid. 'Well you'd better get yourself sorted out. I've got a very important job for you. Our whole future may depend on it.'

'You don't have to look at me when you're talking,' I say.

'Not when you're driving at seventy through a shopping precinct.'

Sid eases his foot off the accelerator. 'I'm going to cut the boys first disc and you're going to see "Mr Fixit".'

'What does he do?' I ask.

'He fixes things,' says Sid.

'I should have thought of that for myself,' I say. 'What sort of things?'

'You know the "Tune for the top" spot on "Pick of the pops"?'

'Some kind of tongue twister, is it?'

'You won't have a tongue if you don't watch it,' says Sid. 'Mr Fixit can make sure that your record gets played on the "Tune for the top" spot. A plug like that helps sell thousands of records.'

'Not bribery?' I say, my breathless tone of voice giving some indication of the deep sense of shock and moral outrage that I feel.

'That's a nasty word, Timmo,' says Sid, all super-cool.

'Not as nasty as phlegm,' I say.

Sid closes his eyes and I have to give him a sharp dig in the ribs.

'Sometimes I worry about you,' he says, narrowly avoiding a milk float.

'And you!' I shout to the driver.

'Now listen,' says Sid. 'I want you to go round and see Mr Fixit and show him that review in the *Guardian*. Tell him about the record and say we'd be grateful for a few plugs.'

'Surely he's going to want more than gratitude, Sid?'

'Of course he will. But we don't have anything to give him, do we? You'll have to offer him a slice of the group.'

'Blimey, there's going to be nothing left in a minute!'

'Don't start that again!' warns Sid. 'Just get round there and do like I say.' It is no good remonstrating with him because I don't know what it means, I sit quietly and think about Bindy Philips. What a fantastic bird she was. She had one of the softest—

'Here we are,' says Sid. 'Now get out there and do your stuff.' I take a shufti out of the window and see that we have stopped outside a tasty terrace house with a yellow front door and a couple of shrubs in tubs adding greenery to the scenery. It is all very nice as obviously thinks the moggy currently engaged in poisoning the privet. I ring the front door bell and turn to see Sid disappearing round the corner. When there is gelt to be felt Sid does not hang about.

'Hi there,' the guy who has opened the door is wearing a velvet suit and a welcoming smile. He grabs my hand in both of his and squeezes my elbow. It is funny but he does not look like Billy Graham. 'Great to see you.'

'Timothy Lea,' I stutter.

'Luxembourg,' he says, 'what can I get you to drink?'

The Luxembourg bit has me a bit confused but I like the rest of it. 'A light ale would slip down a treat,' I say.

'I don't know if we've got any of that,' says the geezer. Maybe he meant that his name was Luxembourg? It's not the kind of thing you want to take a chance on, though is it?'

'A brown, then,' I say, showing him that I am as adaptable as I am sophisticated.

'I think you've got me there, too,' says the bloke. 'Let's go upstairs and join the ladies. I'm certain they'll be able to provide just what you want.' He gives me a big wink and I wonder what he is on about. He has a sort of American accent and is obviously a very friendly bloke. If this is how the Yanks do business, I like it.

We pad up a flight of stairs and into a room where there are three birds in cocktail dresses and a couple of blokes. The birds are wonderful advertisements for the concept of sexual intercourse but it is one of the blokes who attracts my attention most. Gerry Valium! What a coincidence. The famous D.J. and pop personality who gave Kipper their rave review. He will be able to give Mr Fixit a first hand account of how blooming marvellous they are. With a bit of luck I might be able to hang on to the slice of the action I was supposed to use as payola. Sid will be pleased.

'You know Gerry and Marvin?'

A hand is waved in the direction of the two guys and I realise that Marvin is Marvin Dangler, famous D.J. and supermarket opener. I can see why he usually wears dark glasses.

'Of course.' There is a jangle of gold bracelets and the boys wiggle their fingers at me. They both have expressions on their faces like they are waiting for the other one to stop talking so they can say something.

'Are you finding lots of good material these days?' The bird who has addressed me is shaped like a bowl of fruit and her bristols are practically clambering out of her dress. Between my legs, percy starts to twitch like a tiger's tail.

'I'm still wearing a lot of denim,' I say. 'How about you?'

The bird looks puzzled and then smiles. 'You're joking, aren't you?' she says.

'Just a little bit.' I say. 'Any chance of a drink?'

'Of course. I am sorry. Champagne all right?' Before I can say anything the bird has frisked off. They do themselves proud, don't they? I must find a moment to have a word with Mr Fixit, or Luxembourg, or whatever his name is. Probably not a good time to do it with the two D.J.s about.

'Have you heard Spoke Axle's single?' This time the bird is the long thin variety with a dimple that goes right down to her belly button. Her lips are moist and shiny.

'I didn't even know he was married.' I say.

'It's worth playing,' murmurs the bird.

I have never been one to disagree with a thought like that but it seems a funny thing to suddenly come out with. There is something strange about the whole set-up. I wish I could put my finger on it.

'We're going next door, now, Franky,' says the third bird. 'See you.'

'Au revoir, girls.' The bloke who let me in, opens the door with a flourish and the birds sweep out.

'I took it in to the garage and the mechanic looked for the engine in the boot,' says Valium, waving his empty glass like a distress signal. 'It takes so long to get spares that the model has usually been withdrawn by the time they get here.'

'I know just how you feel,' says Dangler sympathetically. 'I've got everybody in the family a Rolls and had done with it.'

'More champagne, old sport?' Franky does not wait for an answer but starts glugging into my glass. I don't fancy the stuff over much but you can't be rude, can you?

'I think we need a little more light on the subject.'

I nod agreeably and watch Franky press a switch on the wall – it's the best place for them. Saves an awful lot of bending. To my amazement, the mirror in front of me suddenly turns into a window. It happens so fast I can hardly believe my eyes. One moment I am staring moodily at my own sensuous reflection, the next, I can see the three birds who were in the room with us. They must be next door. The short, curvy one is standing at the bottom of a giant bed. As I watch she turns her back towards the tall one who starts to unzip her.

'Charming, isn't it?' Franky corrects the angle of my

glass with his finger and turns to the other two blokes who are talking about gear ratios.

Big tits has stepped out of her dress and all three birds are shredding threads like they are going out of fashion. I shouldn't watch but somehow I reckon that is just what I am supposed to bc doing. The tall judy peels off her tights and lays on the bed and the bint who announced that they were all going next door snuggles down beside her. Phew! It's a good job I read the *Daily Telegraph.* If you came from a sheltered background you could get a few nasty shocks these days. Jumbo tits has found something under the pillow and – no! There are limits beyond which I dare not go for risk of offending the more sensitive of my readers. It is all I can do to force myself to watch, let alone actually describe the adventures of that particular piece of pink plastic.

'Do you feel like popping next door?' says Franky.

If I watch much more of that I will be popping just where I am. Blimey! They don't half come on strong, those birds.

'The differential was all to cock.' Valium is loosening his tie like he is about to have a medical check up. He seems about as worked up as a nightwatchman in a bromide factory.

'Leave your clothes in here if you feel like a bit of exercise,' says Franky helpfully.

Marvin Dangler is draping his trousers over the settee so he does not spoil the crease. I notice that he does not undo the knot in his tie, merely loosens it.

'Don't let the champagne get warm,' he says.

Now is probably a good moment to talk to Mr Fixit about Kipper. Both the D.J.'s are beginning to move next door and we will soon be alone.

'Mr – er-er-Franky.' I begin.

'Get your trousers off and get in there,' says my host, patting me on the shoulder.

'I've got a wonderful group.' I say.

'Congratulations. I'll look out for it.'

'I don't think you quite understand what I mean.' I say. 'I—'

Next door, Valium is lying on the bed and the bird with the big boobs is leaning over him like the eve of the grape harvest. The other two birds are helping Dangler off with his pants – they look more like gran's bloomers. It seems wrong somehow, that these brave sons of Albion should go into the fray outnumbered.

'I'll tell you about it later,' I say, 'Do you mind hanging up my Y-fronts?'

CHAPTER SIX

In which Kipper cut their first disc and Timmy shares a disconcerting experience with a lady and some eels at a press reception at Billingsgate Fish Market.

'It didn't work out quite the way I thought it would, Sid,' I whine.

'Not another cock up?' snarls Clapham's low grade Lew Grade.

'It's funny you should say that.' I tell him all about the strange happenings at Mr Fixit's house and the unforseen demands that were made upon personable percy. Also the embarrassment caused when a gentleman turned up who said he was me – or rather that I was pretending to be him. I was very delicately balanced at that particular point and it is fortunate that no permanent damage was done when they threw me down the steps.

'Gordon Bennett!' shrieks Sid. 'I'm slaving my guts out trying to get a recording session fixed up and you're on the nest with a bunch of tarts. That's nice, isn't it?'

'It wasn't bad,' I say. 'I had to bear the brunt, though. The other two geezers weren't exactly Olympic class stamina-wise.'

'I'm going to bear your brunt if you don't get a grip on yourself,' shouts Sid. 'Do you mean to tell me that you didn't even raise the subject?'

'It was difficult to get a word in edgeways,' I say. 'In fact, sometimes it was—'

'Belt up! I'm going to wash my hands of you – and I hope you've done the same. All our problems could have been over if you'd used your nut.'

'I didn't feel I knew them well enough, Sid.'

'I didn't mean that.' Sid runs his fingers through his

barnet. 'I suppose you realise what was happening in there?'

'Most of the time I did. Sometimes it got a bit confusing. I think it was the wrirring noise the camera made. I found—'

'Those two disc-jockey blokes were getting a bit of how's-your-father to encourage them to plug the right tunes, weren't they? Mr Fixit obviously thought you were one of them.'

'Why should he have thought that? There's nothing unusual about the way I dress. Of course, I splash the after shave about a bit, but—'

'One of the disc jockeys.' Sidney speaks very slowly and I can see the veins on the backs of his clenched fists knotting.

'What are we going to do now, Sid?' I say meekly.

Sid takes a few deep breaths and seems to feel better. 'We'll have to find something a little more oblique,' he says. 'Get our waxing adapted as the intro music for the Epilogue or something like that.'

'When we've got it,' I say.

'I have got it.'

I look at Sid in amazement. Can we be talking about the same thing? 'But you only went round to the studio this morning. Slaving your guts out, that's what you said you were doing.'

'Well, I soon stopped slaving my guts out. It suddenly came to me. What's the point of trying to record these geezers? They'd probably lost their instruments or turn up stoned and pissed. I doubt if half of them can play, anyway.'

I have to admit that there is much wisdom in what Sid says. I don't reckon that any one of them is Queen's Scout material.

'So I thought we'd do it with session musicians.'

'What are they, Sid?'

'They're people who can really play the instruments only they look normal.'

'Seems a good idea, Sid.'

'Then I thought of an even easier way.' My eyes widen admiringly. 'Some of these song writer geezers have got tapes full of stuff they have recorded with session artists. All you have to do is buy a track and get yourself five blokes who know which way up to hold a guitar – though even that's not important these days.'

'But Sid. What happens when they have to play it live?'

'They have to practice a bit. But it doesn't matter too much. The kids scream so loud you can't hear a word anyway. Have you ever been to a Stones concert?'

I don't answer because I am thinking about the whole scheme. It seems a good idea, but surely, if Sid has anything to do with it, there must be something missing?

'What about Nutter?' I say.

'What do you mean?'

'You can't tell me that anybody has recorded the sound of somebody bashing up a piano with their bonce? That's the group's whole raisin dates.' (Raison d'etre? *Ed.*)

'It's being attended to at this very moment,' says Sid loftily. 'I've got a bloke bashing away at a tea chest with a rounders bat. We just lay another track on the tape. It's dead simple. The sound of Nutter's nut will be preserved for posterior.' The right place for it, too, I think to myself. But I don't say anything. I can sense that Sid is in a touchy mood.

'You don't think they're going to mind?'

'Kipper? They wouldn't care if it was the Andrews Sisters doing it as long as the money was coming in.'

'Marvellous, Sid. What do you want me to do?' Sid seems to have difficulty in controlling himself.

'Something that doesn't involve coming into contact with other human beings,' he says eventually. 'Something that will give your giant intellect full reign. I want you to think of a title for Kipper's first hit record.'

'I've already done it,' I say.

Sid smiles like a man acknowledging defeat. 'Amaze me.'

' "I got plenty of nutting." '

Sid smiles again. 'I had to ask, didn't I?' He pats me on the back of the neck with his clenched fist. 'Try thinking up a few more. And while you're at it, have a go at a Christmas song. They're real money spinners, they are. "Rudolph The Red-Nosed Reindeer", "All I Want For Christmas Is My Two Front Teeth" ' – Sid looks at me in a funny sort of way when he says that – ' "When Santa Got Stuck Into Grandma". They've all sold a million – "White Christmas" has sold a hundred million.'

'I think I could be very good at that,' I say.

'I'm certain you could, Timmo. That's why I suggested it. Don't forget, it should be sentimental and a little bit jokey. It helps if it mentions Christmas, too.'

Sid disappears to make the world a better place to live in – provided your name is Sidney Noggett, that is – and I settle down with a sheet of paper and one of those new non-leak, non-smudge fountain pens. When I have cleaned up most of the ink and washed my hands I settle down to the song writing.

The big problem is getting everything in, yet keeping it short. 'I'm Coming Home For Christmas Because I Miss You And The Rabbits,' is strong on sentiment but it does go on a bit. It is also not very funny. 'I'm Coming Home For Christmas Because I Miss Having A Joke With You And The Rabbits,' is no better. In fact the mention of the joke tends to undermine the sentimental mood. It is all very difficult. You can see how smart old Irving Berlin was to call his song 'White Christmas'. It's dead simple and your imagination does all the work. I mean, you only have to mention those words and you immediately start thinking about burst pipes, power cuts, family rows, stomach powders and all the other things that symbolise the festive season.

Maybe there is a lesson for me. 'Nippy Noel', 'Icy Xmas'.

They're not in the same class, are they? Short, but lacking that vital ingredient that you only know is there when you see it. Perhaps I was wrong to abandon the first line of attack so easily.

Rabbits. There is something wrong about rabbits. They are an outdoor animal. I need something warmer. Something nearer home. A cat. That's it! Why didn't I think of that before? 'I'm Coming Home For Christmas Because I Miss Your Pussy'. The minute I see it I know I have got something. Sid is going to be so pleased with me!

In fact, Sid does not even bother to ask me about my songs when he bursts through the door.

'Right,' he says. 'It's all fixed up. I've heard the record and I've told the group. Now it's just a question of the launch party and we're in business.'

'What about the title?' I ask.

'Oh yeah. It's called "Fourteen Times In Twenty-Two Minutes."'

'Why, Sid?' I mean, I feel bitter. Really bitter.

'I dunno. The boys chose it. It means something to them.'

'But Sid. You asked me to—'

Sid waves his hands in my face. 'Don't let's go into that now. There isn't time. We've got to get this launch party organised.' Sometimes I reckon that Sid is going to snuff it with my fingerprints on his wind pipe, and this is one of those moments.

'Where's it going to be?' I say, tight-lipped.

'Billingsgate, of course. Where else could it be for a group called Kipper?'

'You're joking, Sid.'

'No I'm not. I'm dead serious.'

'But what about the pong?'

'We'll get them to wash first.'

'I didn't mean the group, Sid,' I say, trying to keep calm. Honestly, I wonder about him sometimes.

'Oh, the fish. Yeh, well, that's all part of the local colour, isn't it?' Once again, I can see Sid's boyish enthusiasm steering us towards a mammoth cock-up. I mean, I have tremendous respect for all those wonderful people who keep us in plaice, but would you really choose Billingsgate if you were organising a press reception? The fish counter at Harrods maybe. Unfortunately it is impossible to budge Sid once he has got an idea in his nut and soon he is explaining how he is going to send out kipper-shaped invites and serve kipper and chips to the guests. The only good thing I can see about the choice of venue is that none of the guests will be surprised by the language.

Come the big night and it is pissing with rain as I knew it would be. Sid has really splashed out the moola and there are braziers everywhere to keep the guests warm. Sid calls them brassieres which is understandable when you think that he seldom warms his hands on anything else. The guests arrive slowly at first but as closing time approaches a genial crowd of free loaders are to be seen pouring gargle down their throats and telling everybody their plans to take over the world. Trembler, Nutter, Fuggy, Pete and Reg are there to charm everyone with their easy wit and I see Sid sticking to them like a piece of horse shit.

'How do you feel about the world we live in?' asks one elderly gentleman of the press, licking his pencil. Sid tries to reply but Fuggy has obviously been looking forward to expressing his views.

'You don't have to answer for me,' he says. 'Just because I like humping chicks it doesn't mean I'm not deeply interested in pollution of the environment and all that.' He drops a sweet paper on the floor and grimaces. 'These bloody fangs don't half give me gip. I'll be glad when I can replace the bastards with lumps of gold.'

I am heartened to see that the boys are taking such care to project a fresh, unspoilt image. Somebody must have had a word with them.

'Like my head is just vegetable matter,' mumbles Nutter to a bird who is in danger of getting a crick in her neck the way she is looking up into his stupid face. 'I'm right through the piano and into what it's all about. Like wood. You dig? It's the only pure marriage. You can quote me on that. You know how to spell my name? It's G-O-'

'Are you part of this circus?' The voice is as cool as an eskimo's inside leg measurement and belongs to a bird with a Veronica Lake hairstyle and eyes you could drown in. If I had to swim for it I would choose the breast-stroke – her knockers are knock-out.

'I'm part of the management team,' I say modestly.

'You look more like a performer.' The voice is strictly 'come up and see me sometime'.

'I'm a bit past it for that,' I say.

'You amaze me – amaze me and disappoint me.' She breathes out through her hooter and her nostrils vibrate like streamers in an electric fan. Something tells me that she may have an excitable nature.

'You're Press, are you?' I ask.

The bird nods all the way down to her knee caps. '*Meet Market*,' she says. 'The organ of committed communication between thinking groovers.'

'You publish all those letters, don't you?' I say, hoping I don't sound too interested. 'I often wonder if—'

'They're all authentic,' says the bird, answering my question. 'You have to be very inhibited to doubt it.'

'Just what I thought,' I say hurriedly. 'I don't find anything strange about it – well, I suppose the bird who used to order a second pint of milk on Fridays because—'

'She was unusual.' Agrees the lady. 'But not to be censored.'

'Oh, of course not. It just seemed that with this shortage of milk bottles—'

'Society is there to serve the needs of the individual.'

'The Co-op, you mean? Yes I suppose you're right. We have United Dairies, I think. I can't really remember.'

The bird looks at me in a funny sort of way. 'You're a a strange young man. Were you breast fed?'

I feel myself go scarlet. What a thing to say. And there are fish porters only a few yards away. I flatter myself that I am fairly broad-minded but – really, there is a limit.

'I don't know,' I say, looking round nervously. 'I expect my Mum would, but she isn't here.'

'I don't think you could have been,' says the bird. 'Otherwise you wouldn't be so fascinated by them. You haven't taken your eyes off mine since I've been talking to you.'

'That's not true,' I say. 'Here, let me get you a pair of knockers – I mean a drink!' I practically scream the last four words and the bloke standing next to me drops the serviette-full of sausage rolls he is trying to cram into his jacket pocket.

'I'm Harriette Gibson and I'd like to help you,' says the bird.

'Timothy Lea – and beware of imitations,' I say. 'I'm sorry. I'll get you that drink.'

'I don't want a drink. I want to talk to you.' She sounds like she has a syringe hidden behind her back.

'There's nothing wrong with me,' I say. 'I'm just not feeling my breast – I MEAN BEST!!'

Harriette squeezes the inside of my leg sympathetically.

'Poor boy. You're very inhibited, aren't you?'

'I wouldn't have said that,' I say, trying to think about it.

'It's nothing to be ashamed of. Very few of us ever achieve total mastery over our sexual repressions. We're often terrified by the magnitude of our desires. The sexual innovator is always at the mercy of the least dominant of the species.'

'Yes,' I say. I don't have the faintest idea what she is rabbiting about but I like to sound positive.

Harriette sniffs. 'That smell. What does it remind you of?'

'Fish?' I say.

'It *is* fish,' says Harriette, firmly. 'I asked you what it *reminded* you of.'

'More fish?'

'You don't like reality, do you, Timothy?' Miss Gibson takes one of my hands and guides it towards a shapely knocker. Fortunately it belongs to her.

'Now and then,' I say.

'Let's go for a walk. This is such a fascinating place.' I don't reckon it all that much myself. Away from the piss-up it is dark and damp and the niff doesn't exactly remind you of the inside of a perfume factory.

'They're going to do the song in a minute,' I say.

'I only like progressive music.' Miss Gibson's mits enjoy another thigh-level revel. 'I'm a very progressive girl.'

'I think you'll find them very progressive,' I breathe.

'It's you I'm interested in,' husks my new friend. 'Let's make our own music.' I don't know what instrument she is used to playing but I can't help having a few ideas. Her pinkies race over my zipper like it is a midget xylophone.

'Maybe we should be going back now,' I say. 'You don't want to miss anything.'

'Exactly.'

Before I can shout for help she has thrown herself onto my mush like it is the last bus home and is kissing me passionately. What a funny woman.

'Let it all hang out,' she says, wrenching open my flies. 'Abandon yourself to your heart's desires. Revel in shameless lust!' She does go on a bit, doesn't she? I always seem to be bumping into these excitable women. It must have something to do with their glands.

'Careful!' I say. 'You'll have us both in the eels.' There, at our feet, is a sunken pit full of eels. They are knotted up like a tin of worms and the sight puts me right off my Ovaltine – back home I even have to get Mum to thread my shoe laces.

'Aren't they beautiful?' breathes Miss G. 'Big and black and thick and slippery.' Her eyes are gleaming in the darkness. Very spooky it is. 'What do they remind you of?' She has another go at the front of my trousers and this time I reckon she is souvenir hunting. A few more smash and grab raids like that and I'll be auditioning for the Vienna Boys Choir.

'Snakes,' I say. I don't reckon she can argue with me there. They don't look like bleeding hampsters.

'I want to do it down there,' she says, all strained-like.

'O.K. I'll look the other way,' I say. I mean, I'm a gent when it comes to that kind of thing. I was brought up to show respect to a lady. I always lift the seat when we are in the karsi together.

'I mean, I want to have sex with you down there.' She hisses. 'Imagine the sensations. A thousand big, black—'

'Don't!' I can hardly bear to think about it. This bird reminds me of the one who had a go at me in the coal cellar. Mrs Evans, I think here name was. It probably had something to do with her Welsh blood.

'Don't be shy, Timothy. Live your dreams.'

That's my trouble, I suppose. I don't have dreams like that. I don't think a lot of blokes do. But birds – now there's another kettle of fish, if you'll excuse the expression. They have a lot of *very* funny ideas flitting through their nuts. They don't go on about it as much as blokes but on the whole I reckon they are much more depraved. This one certainly is, anyway. She is wriggling out of her dress before you can say 'Battersea Dogs' Home' and making noises like feeding time at the reptile house.

'I think I'd better be getting back,' I say. Somewhere behind me I can hear the sound of splintering wood and I know they must be playing our song. I haven't heard it yet and – 'OY!!' By the cringe but she is strong this girl. She grabs my arm as I turn to go and with a gurgling shriek of liberated ecstasy, drags me into the pit. I have no intention of staying there but have you ever tried to sprint over half a ton of eels? It's no picnic I can tell you.

'Surrender to your instincts!' yelps Miss Gibson. I am

screaming too, but mainly because an eel has just gone up my trouser leg. I mean, they are a bit free with their teeth, aren't they? And they like worms. Help! 'That's better,' breathes Hungry Harriette. 'You're beginning to feel it now, aren't you?'

I am beginning to wonder if I will ever feel it again. The stupid bag has misunderstood my reasons for jumping six feet in the air and is now ripping off my trousers.

'Let me have it,' she gasps. 'Aaaaaaaargh!'

I don't know what she is on about. I mean, percy is still pointing out the fanlight to my goolies. Why is she—? Oh dear. I think she must have made a mistake. The light is certainly very bad. I can't believe that she meant to – no, she can't have done. Maybe I should say something? No, better not. It might upset her.

With a happy sigh Miss G. falls back onto the rest of the eels and I start emptying the water out of my turn-ups. I can see it is going to be one of those evenings.

CHAPTER SEVEN

In which Timmy and Sid go to unusual lengths to crash the hit parade and Timmy makes a new friend in Mr Dronge's office.

'Next time you have an idea for a publicity stunt you talk to me about it.' Sid bashes his fist against the paper. 'It's no bleeding good me trying to tone down their image if you organise naked chicks to run all over the place.'

'I'm sorry, Sid,' I say.

Sid tries to look fatherly. 'I appreciate you trying to show initiative for a change – but why eels? You should have had the bird with a necklace of kippers if you were going to do anything.'

'It wasn't that carefully worked out,' I say. I am not kidding, either. It was a complete surprise to me when the porter turned the hose on Harriette. It's the last place you would expect to find a lay friar, isn't it? A fish fryer, maybe, but—

'Next time. Do work it out. This kind of stuff isn't going to do us any good at all.' He waves a headline in front of me which reads "Naked Harriette sparks off sex orgy riot". 'You know how excitable they are.'

'I'm sorry, Sid. But you can't blame me for what happened in the eel pit. I didn't tell them all to jump in and—'

' "Stars on Sunday" is right up the spout, now.' Moans Sid. 'I could see them up there sitting on the right hand of Cliff Richard.'

'You're just a dreamer, Sid. Look on the bright side. We got a lot of free publicity. That was what it was all about, wasn't it?'

'I suppose you're right.' Sid sighs and pushes away the papers. '*Melody Maker* are going to do an "in depth probe" on them and the record should be in the shops now. Catchy little number, isn't it?'

'I haven't heard it yet,' I say. 'I've been thinking about those Christmas tunes and I—'

'We haven't got time for that now,' says Sid hurriedly. 'There's work to be done.'

'What do we do now, Sid? Once the record is in the shops we just have to hope that someone buys it, don't we?'

Sid shakes his head slowly. 'Your knavety is touching sometimes. We have to get the record out of the shops. You've heard of the hit parade, haven't you? If nobody buys us, we're not in it. And if we're not in it, nobody buys us. In other words, if we're not in it, we're right in it. Do I make myself clear?'

'I think so, Sid. You mean we've got to organise a few plugs to get the record into the charts?'

Sid looks round carefully to see if we are being overheard and beckons me towards him. Since we are sitting in Mum's kitchen at Scraggs Lane I think he is overdoing it a bit.

'We can go further than that,' he murmurs. 'How do you think the Hit Parade works?'

'They find out from the shops which records are selling best.'

'Exactly, Timmo. You're not just a diabolically ugly face, are you? But they don't ask all the shops, just a selected number. You see what that means?'

'Of course,' I say.

'No you don't,' says Sid. 'But don't worry. I'm going to tell you. It means that if you know which shops they're using, you can nip round there and buy enough records to put your song in the charts.'

'But how do you know which shops they're using?'

Sid taps his nose. I have friends. A nod is as good as a wank to a blind whore.

'I should think it is,' I say, wincing. 'But surely you can't just wander in there and buy a couple of hundred copies of

"Sixteen Times In Twenty-Two Minutes". Somebody is going to smell a rat.'

'"Fourteen times",' says Sid. 'Try and get the bleeding title right. You're going to be asking for it enough times.'

'Me?'

'That's right. You just answered your own question. Of course, one bloke can't go in and buy hundreds of records. The whole family is going to have to work at it.'

'It's going to cost a bit, Sid.'

Sid puts on his patient, 'How To Make Your First Million' face. 'Timmy boy. If I've told you once I've told you a hundred times. You've got to put it in to get it out. If we only get our money back on the first record I'm not worried. It's establishing the group that's important. By the time we get to record number three it'll be a hit before it gets into the shops.' You have to hand it to Sid, don't you? Talk about the bulldog spirit. It doesn't matter what kind of pasting he's taken, he always rushes back for another mouthful of boot.

'There's only one thing I'm worried about,' I say.

'Yes,' says Sid. 'I'm worried about him too. But we've got to use the stupid old git. We need every hand we can get.'

As if responding to some magic summons Dad enters the kitchen carrying a couple of gas masks. 'Just going to change the crystals,' he says.

'Why worry? The rubber is all perished.'

'They'll come in handy, don't you worry.' Says Dad knowingly. Dad has been waiting for the Chinese invasion for some years now and has also flirted with the idea of converting the gas masks into long-life breathalysers. Unfortunately, for reasons best known to themselves, nobody in the family is prepared to convey the idea to the Fuzz. Personally, I think he was wrong to cut a hole for his pipe, but it is a waste of time talking to him.

'How would you like to make a bit of beer money, Dad?' says Sid.

'Honestly,' says Dad, revealing his salty wit. 'And there's

precious little chance of doing that if you two spongers are tied up with something.'

'That's very nice coming from a geezer who kits out his home with stuff knocked off from the lost property office,' says Sid.

Dad's face turns a delicate shade of mauve. 'How dare you inseminate that I'm a tea leaf,' he says. 'If I ever brought anything home it was only to save it from being cremated.'

'That's morbid,' says Sid. 'It shows you how his mind works. It dwells on death.'

'It dwells on some deaths.' Dad gives Sid what might be termed an old-fashioned look. Some sixth sense tells me that agrochat is lurking round the corner and I am glad when Mum arrives to ask if anyone would like dinner. This is always the signal for the kitchen to be cleared faster than a dynamite factory in a bomb scare. Sid and I lock shoulders in the doorway. I won't say that Mum's cooking is bad but the last shepherd's pie she made had pieces of smock in it. Her meals are like dangerous pills. It is advisable not to take more than two a day.

Fortunately we managed to get Dad round the boozer and a few light and milds later he is getting quite enthusiastic about buying records.

'Silver Threads Amongst The Gold,' he says. 'That was a record. I remember it like it was yesterday.'

'It was yesterday,' says Sid. 'You told Mum not to play it because she was ruining the needle.'

'Silver threads amongst the gold,' warbles Dad. 'You and I are getting o-o-o-o-ld!'

'Gordon Bennett,' says Sid. 'Let's get him out of here. They'll be taking a hat round in a minute.'

When it comes to the crunch, Dad is not unsympathetic to the idea of a few oncers lining his jacket pocket and it is no problem lining up Mum and one or two of my aunties. Rosie is less enthusiastic but that is Sid's problem. He can work on her and the staff of Plonkers.

'Your lot can concentrate on the Smoke and I'll nip up to Brum and one or two of the other northern cities,' he says. 'We want to spread it around a bit.' That is one of Sid's problems. He thinks Leeds United Reserves play at Potter's Bar. I have never met a bloke who was more London oriented – not to mention Leyton Oriented. 'Try and keep a grip on your old man,' he pleads. 'If he cocks this up I'll swing for him.'

With these words of encouragement he stamps off to pack his over-night bag. Thinking of over-night bags makes me wonder which little piece of tottie filled him in about the record shops. There is a woman in it somewhere or my name is not Timothy Lea.

As he gets older, Sid plays his sexual adventures much closer to the nut-chokers and does not rabbit on as much as he used to. I don't think he wants to give Rosie any more cause for carrying on than he has to.

Sid reckons that we need a week to do the job properly and I have a little list of the shops we have got to cover. Each day each of us is going to a different round of shops so that we don't make the staff suspicious. I share Sid's misgivings about Dad and these appear to be well justified. Giving Dad a large helping of moola is like handing a junkie the key to the medicine cabinet. He gets on the job just before opening time and starts again when they close.

'We should have given him record tokens,' I say to Sid.

'He'd still have changed them for beer,' says Sid.

'Handel's lager,' I say.

Sid stares at me blankly. Sometimes I wish I had Robin Ray for a brother in law. Mum is much more dependable but I have to speak to her when she comes back with a disc down the side of her string-bag full of potatoes.

'They're going to think it a bit odd if you just bung them in with the spuds,' I say. 'You want to sound like a real enthusiast.'

'I don't know about that,' says Mum. 'I had enough trouble getting the record. The girl asked if they were on a casette. I thought that was some kind of ice cream.'

I decide to concentrate on Dad.

It is as well I do because when I am in Deadly Dave's Dynamic Discount Drive the assistant is quick to remark that 'Fourteen Times In Twenty-Two Minutes' has been creating a lot of interest.

'This old man came in and bought fifteen of them,' she says. 'He kicked up an awful fuss because we wouldn't give him an extra discount. He said he was buying them for an old peoples' home. He was a horrible old man—'

'Yeh. I can imagine,' I say hurriedly. 'There's a lot of them about.' I scarper round to the nearest boozer and, sure enough, there is the rotten old sod supping his pint amongst a pile of beer-spattered discs.

'They're not beer mats, you know,' I say bitterly – no joke intended. It just slipped out, as the actress said to the bishop.

'Well they should be,' says Dad. 'Those little holes in the middle drain the beer away a treat.'

'Don't change the subject,' I hiss. 'What do you mean by wandering about buying stacks of records at one go?'

'It saves time,' whines Dad. 'They're not going to suspect anything. I said they were for a youth club.'

'Gordon Bennett! How many records have you got?' I look down on the floor and there is a dirty great pile of discs threatening to bury his ankles.

'Don't round on me, son. I'm trying to do my best.' Dad turns up the volume and manages to get a break in his voice. I would like to get one in his neck. Unfortunately, the boozer is chocker with senior citizens and they are swift to offer protection to one of their own.

'Leave the old man alone,' says a geezer with a mug like a deflated football. 'You push off and buy your own records.'

'You tell him, Arthur,' says another interfering old ratbag.

'Young people today have got no respect.'

'Sweated and slaved . . .' mumbles Dad. 'Never wanted for anything . . . All I get is abuse . . . Can't go on . . .'

By the time I get to the door the whole lot of them are snuffling in their beer and I have been threatened with a Dr Barnardo's box. There is nothing for it but to get back on the beat – blimey, I keep making these diabolical jokes without meaning to.

I am doubly choked by Dad's attitude because I have been bending over backwards not to give the game away. When I return to the shop I often buy another record with my own money so the assistant does not get suspicious. It is very difficult because I do not want to give some other bastard a leg up the charts, and they don't do the classics on forty-fives – not with the same arrangement, anyway.

It is while I am standing in the big store in the High Street that I meet Georgie. She strolls around pretending she isn't waiting for you to nick a pair of headphones, and looking bored in a fanciable sort of way.

'I'd like "An Unnatural Kind Of Loving", "Fourteen Times In Twenty-Two Minutes", and "No Questions Asked",' I say.

'Yerwhat?'

The bird looks quite taken aback. I suppose I do speak a bit fast sometimes. I'm frightened, you see.

'Those three records,' I say, trying to get it back to $33\frac{1}{3}$.

'Oh yeh.' The bird starts reaching in the shelf behind her.

'You've been here before, haven't you?'

'On and off,' I say. Has she remembered what I bought? Does she suspect something? Will Tarzan escape from the pit full of tarantulas?

'I know why you come,' she says. I do not think that she is trying to steer the conversation round to a discussion of reproductory processes. She must have rumbled me! 'It's because of Sacha, isn't it?' She jerks her head towards a good looking bird down the end of the counter.

'I hadn't noticed her till you pointed her out,' I lie. 'If I had to make the choice, I'd choose you every time.'

'She's always got blokes going up to her and asking her out.' The bird is feeding me a lot of eye and quiver and it occurs to me that she is responding to my brute animal magnetism. Ah well, you can't fault her taste.

'I don't see it myself,' I say. 'I mean, she's a good looking girl but not, well, not in your class.'

'You must be the only bloke in the world who thinks that,' she says with justifiable modesty.

'I don't think so,' I say in a voice drenched with sincerity. 'I like bones, you see.' The lady has a schonk so big you could use it for prising off hub caps.

'You really think I'm attractive?' says the bird.

'What time do you have your dinner break?' I say. I mean there is a queue forming behind us and if I don't get out soon they are going to be the first to hear of our engagement.

'Half past twelve.'

'I'll buy you a coffee.' I waggle my fingers at her and glide away like David Niven on roller skates. Sometimes I feel I ought to take ugly pills. It is just not fair to the rest of the blokes. It is only when I get outside that I find I have left the records on the counter. Silly Timothy Lea! Now I will have to go and take Miss Hooter out for a cup of instant. Not that the prospect is too unappealing. The bird is well assembled and anything that fancies you can't be bad, can it? I mean, I'm not going to wait for Sophia Loren to take English lessons if there is some little raver trying to see the colour of my Y-fronts. It stands to reason, doesn't it?

I visit a couple more shops and am back on the stroke of twelve thirty. Miss Bracket makes a command performance of sweeping across to me and I can see that she is as thrilled as she ought to be.

'I think the cafes are going to be very crowded around here,' I say. 'Why don't we have a quick snort in the boozer? It'll warm you up a treat.'

'I don't usually drink at dinner-time,' says the bird. 'Spirits go right through me.' Something tells me that they are not the only ones but I keep the thought to myself. Few birds have much of a sense of humour, especially when it comes to a spot of in-and-out.

'Just this once,' I say, coaxingly. I read somewhere that a bloke's sexual drive is at its peak early in the morning. Mine must of had a bit of a lay-in today. I have suddenly got a touch of the white hots for the bird. If I had somewhere to take her I reckon I could be in like Flynn.

'You will look after me, won't you,' she says.

'Have no fear, Tim is here,' I say. I settle her down in 'The Lamb and Cuspidor' and set her up with a Babycham. Hang the expense, I say. What's the point of being alive if you can't splash it about a bit? I don't know the meaning of the word austerity – to name but just one word.

'You don't think my nose is too big?' says the bird.

'Never,' I say, trying to lean round it to attract the barmaid's attention. 'Fancy a packet of crisps?'

'Ta.'

I can see that she is impressed by the way that expense appears to be no object. It's little touches like that that make all the difference with birds. I used to think that Sid had it, but he does not know his savoir faire from his bus fare.

'I think you're a very, very attractive girl,' I say. Take my advice. With women, never use a trowel if there's a spade handy.

'I think you're nice, too,' says the bird. 'I thought so from the very first time you came in. I never thought you'd notice me.'

I give a little laugh as if the whole idea is too ridiculous for words.

'I could hardly take my eyes off you,' I say. 'The trouble is that I'm so shy. I couldn't screw up the courage to speak to you.'

'You did look shy,' agrees my new admirer. 'Mr Dronge thought you were a shop lifter.'

'I don't look that strong, do I?' I say, showing her that I am witty as well as worldly. She laughs like a drain to show me that she hasn't the faintest idea what I'm talking about and I nonchalantly blow the froth off my pint.

'Sorry,' I say. I get out a handkerchief and then put it away again. If you use them when the chain comes off your bike they are never the same, are they?

She wipes her blouse and smiles. 'We haven't even introduced ourselves, have we? I'm Georgie Lane.'

'Timothy Lea.' I gaze deep into her eyes like we are having a 'first one to blink is a cissy' competition and knock off a heart-rending sigh. 'It's funny, but I feel a tremendous physical attraction for you. I suppose I've felt it from the first moment I saw you.'

I touch her hand and she grabs it like it was running past her down a steep hill. 'Me too.'

'Let's go somewhere,' I say all excited and breathless as if the idea has just occurred to me.

'But where?'

Knickers! I hoped she was going to answer that one.'

'They've taken all the doors off the cubicles.'

Vandals!! Screams my inner voice.

'We might go in Mr Dronge's office. He always goes to the branch meeting on Wednesdays.'

'Let's do that,' I say, sinking my pint so fast it doesn't touch the inside of my throat.

'Just for a chat.'

'Naturally.' You know, birds are very funny like that. They always have to make it look like the last thing they were thinking about. When I was window cleaning I remember a dolly who met me in the hall in a negligee and then acted amazed that the electric blanket had been turned on.

We waltz back to the shop and I am thinking about it so much I can hardly keep the chat going.

'We can get in the back way,' says Georgie. 'I don't want the others to see us. Not that we're going to do anything wrong, of course.'

'Of course not.' This is another funny thing about birds. They tell their mates every detail, but they never want them to know beforehand. We don't have to go into the showroom to get into the office and I breathe a sigh of relief as the door clicks shut behind us.

'The lock doesn't work. You'll have to wedge a chair under the handle.' I wonder how she knows that? Maybe her relationship with Mr Dronge is closer than that which normally exists between boss and employee.

'You have wonderful eyes,' I say. My voice sounds so sincere that for a moment I think there is someone else in the room.

'Do you think so?'

Women are so selfish, aren't they? You pay a bird a compliment and all they say is 'ta' or 'This old thing? I've had it for years.' They never think of saying anything nice to say about you. When was the last time some bird said 'Cedric, my precious one, you don't half have beautifully shaped lug holes' or the like? I bet it was bleeding years ago.

'I have a strange hunger for you,' I say. It is always favourite if you make it sound as if some secret force has liberated natural impulses which you are unable to resist. If you put your mit up their skirt you are inclined to cop a slap round the mush, if your natural forces do it then it is all right. 'I must have you.' This is no lie. Down where my body splits in two, percy craves action. Having lost out to an unlikely contender at Billingsgate he is determined not to be robbed of his prey this time.

Fortunately, Georgie Lane does not seem to be the kind of girl to prevent anybody's hampton enjoying a spot of innocent fun. No sooner have I inclined my head towards hers than she is bustling against me like a spring tide. Her mouth finds mine like it has homed onto it by radar and her powerful lips force me back against Mr Dronge's desk. Am I going to take this lying down? The answer seems to be yes. Mr Dronge keeps a very untidy desk and I don't fancy having a playful prod between the groaning in-trays. I start popping open the buttons of Georgie's blouse and – brrrrh! brrrrrh!, brrrrh! brrrrrrh! The noise has nothing to do with her knockers. It comes from the telephone.

'Leave it,' I murmur. 'No! I mean the telephone.'

It is a pity because I was quite enjoying what she was doing to my spam ram.

'I can't.' She says. She picks up the receiver and I hear a muffled voice crashing through the sound waves.

'Hello. I'd like to order a copy of "Fifteen Times In Twenty-Eight Minutes".' There is a loud hic-cupping noise and a berp. 'The address is, Eighty, Nightingale Lane.' There is a noise like someone falling off a bar stool and the line goes dead.

'That's funny,' says Georgie. 'That was one of the records you had.'

'Amazing,' I husk. 'Like that perfume you're wearing. It's sen-sat-ion-al.' With every syllable I slide my mit further up her inside leg measurement. Some birds jump on your wrist faster than a pair of handcuffs with legs, but not this one. She rubs her knockers against my chest and – brrrrh! brrrrrh!, brrrrh! brrrrrrh! – oh my gawd! How much more can a man take?

'Hello. I'd like fourteen and sixpence worth for twenty-three bob.' The voice does not sound a lot different from last time – just more relaxed. 'Forty-five, Scraggs Lane.' That is where Seretse Khan and his lovely life Mabel live. Strange, but it did not seem like either of them. Seretse went to Harrow and his wife is Chinese.

'Don't answer it again,' I plead. 'It's having a bad effect on our love affair.'

'I don't know what to put down,' says Georgie, chewing her pencil.

'I know what I'd like you to put up,' I say – O.K. so it's

not vintage Noel Coward, but what do you expect for 35p – C. P. Snow?

'You're wicked,' she scolds.

'You'll have to take me in hand,' I murmur.

'Like this?'

'That's *very* good.' Her fingers are racing round my action man kit like they are trying to break a speed-typing record. What a bird. I duck under her hooter and we meld mouths again.

'Let's get on the floor,' I breathe.

'I thought you'd never ask.' Like migrating swallows her dainty fingers bid a temporary farewell to my hampton and she sinks slowly to the floor. With a half smile playing round her cakehole, she looks me straight in the mince pies and starts to tug up her skirt. I think she is trying to tell me something. With percy quivering like an unexploded bomb I step out of my jeans and – brrrrrh! brrrh!, brrr – the receiver jumps into my hand.

'Hellosh. This ish Buckingham Polish. I want—'

'Piss off, Dad!!!' I scream into the mouthpiece. There is a strangled groan and a sound like someone falling heavily from a bar stool before the lines goes dead.

'It was a wrong number,' I say, replacing the receiver in a bowl of plastic tulips. 'Don't go away I think this one could go straight to the top.'

CHAPTER EIGHT

In which Kipper appear – fleetingly – on Pick Of The Pops and Timmy and Sid help Sadies Ladies overcome an unexpected problem.

By the end of the week the family home is knee-deep in records. You can't move without sending another pile crashing to the floor. We must have nearly two thousand. Sid is surprised that there were so many.

'They must have printed more than they said they were going to,' says Sid. 'If you lot stuck to the list of names I gave you there should have been about half this number.'

'They probably printed some more because of the demand,' I say.

Sid's face brightens. 'Yes. I hadn't thought of that. It doesn't really matter, anyway. They're all our records.'

'They make nice place mats, don't they?' says Mum.

'Dad has already thought of that,' I tell her.

Dad is not with us round the breakfast table, having been confined to his bed with an attack of an incurable bone disease he suffers from. It is known as bone idleness. He may also be recovering from the effects of a fall sustained when he collapsed outside the public bar of the Lamb and Cuspipor. He was just passing by, of course.

'What are you smiling at?' says Sid.

'We've got all these records and yet I've never heard the song that will soon be blasting its way into the hit parade.'

'We can soon take care of that,' says Sid. 'Where's the record player, Mum?' 'In the front room, dear. But be careful with it. It's never been the same since Rosie tried to cast pots on it.'

'Typical, isn't it?' says Sid a couple of minutes later as he tries to chip the clay off the turn-table. 'She's just the same today. She gets these enthusiasms and then it's all over in a couple of weeks.' Poor old Sid, I think to myself. You were one of the first of them, mate.

'This one didn't last that long,' I say. 'You can still see the marks on the wall where the clay hit it. Dad got one load smack in the kisser.'

'Pity it hadn't turned into a vase,' says Sid. 'Right. Fold back your lug holes. Here it comes, the sound of the seventies, Kipperfection – that's what I'm going to call the L.P.'

'Very good, Sid.' Can this be it? Have I at last arrived at the gates of the vault? Are all my troubles over?

Sid lowers the record arm and –

'Tiptoe through the tulips, through the tulips—'

'Funny intro,' I say. 'It reminds me of something else.' Sid practically wrenches off the turn-table with the record.

'It must have got mixed up with our lot by mistake,' he says. 'Strange. It's got the right label on. Hang on a minute.'

The speed with which he covers the distance between the front room and the kitchen is quite remarkable for a man of his living habits.

'Let's try this one.'

'Come into the garden, Maud.
The black bat, night, has flown.
Come into the garden, Maud.
I am here at the gate alone.'

'I like that bit about the black bat,' I say. 'It's clever. But why is he standing at the gate? Is he the dustman or something?'

'That's not it either, you stupid berk!' hisses Sid. 'Don't you see what's happened? We've been done.'

'I don't get it, Sid.

Sid sinks into an armchair like a lead weight into warm coffee.

'That little scrubber set me up,' he groans. 'They knew we were going round those shops so they got hold of every old record they wanted to get rid of and stuck Bella labels on them.'

'Can't we take them back, Sid?'

'Not two thousand of them! We give ourselves away then and they know it.' Sid grits his teeth and knots his fists. 'It's diabolical! You can't trust nobody, these days.'

'Anybody.' I correct him.

'Belt up! I don't want a bleeding English lesson at a moment like this. Do you realise I've lost going on for a thousand quid? And I haven't even got my own records back. When I think of what I went through to get that info.'

'I can imagine, Sid. It must have been terrible for you. Nice, was she?'

Sid winces. 'I wouldn't have touched her with yours if it hadn't been for Noggo.'

'Poor old Sid. My heart bleeds for you.'

'Your hooter is going to bleed for me and all if you don't stop taking the piss!' Unpleasantness is but seconds away and it is as well that Mum arrives to bring news of an unexpected visitor.

'There's a funny looking fella outside with a green head.' She says. 'I thought he was one of those Green Giant people but he was very rude when I showed him a couple of tins.'

'Bleeding Nutter Normanton. What does he want?' snarls Sid.

Nutter is not slow to tell us, once he has shambled past Mum and rejected a cup of tea – 'I'm right off the laudanum kick, lady. I want out,' he says.

'"Out"? But you've hardly been in,' shrieks Sid.

'Like I'm carrying this whole scene, man.' Mumbles the green freak. 'It's my cultured cranium that people are pay-ing to see. The rest of the guys are just backing me. Who needs them?'

'You mustn't let success go to your head,' I say.

Sid looks at me sharply before continuing. 'Timmy's right,' he says. 'You need the group. You can't just go out there by yourself and smash up pianos with your nut.'

'Not just pianos, man.' Nutter taps Sid on the chest. 'Don't sell me short. I'm an all round entertainer. I can smash up anything. I'm thinking of having a go at an organ.'

'An electric organ?' Sid fights to keep the note of hope out of his voice.

'I don't know yet. It depends how the vibrations buzz me. Know what I mean?' I would not mind so much if he knew how to snap his fingers. You get more sound from rubbing a pair of cleansing pads together.

'Don't be a fool to yourself, Nutter,' says Sid. 'We're on the brink of something really big. Don't start rocking the boat now.'

'You trying to sound like the prime minister or something already?' says the great schmuck. 'The only way I'm going to stay is if I get a bigger slice of the action. It's ridiculous me being paid the same as those other creeps. I'm a star, I take all the risks, my old lady says . . .'

By the time we have got rid of him, Sid and I have only got fourteen per cent between us – and I know the kind of percentage I'm likely to get of that.

'We only need the rest of them in here and we'll be owing them money,' I say. Hardly have the words escaped from my lips than we have Reg 'Short Arse' Sharp on the doorstep.

'Hello, Reggy-boy,' says Sid like he is Father Christmas. 'What do you—'

'More bread,' says Reg. 'I'm carrying this group and I'm not earning enough to buy a new guitar.'

'But you don't need a guitar these days,' says Sid patiently.

Short Arse is not impressed. 'I need to practise so I can get the movements right when I'm not playing,' he says. 'It's not easy standing out there and doing your nut when you've got nothing in your hands.'

'I appreciate that, Reg. But you've got to understand how we stand at the moment. We're very delicately balanced . . .'

Ten minutes later, Short Arse has pushed off and Sid and I have ten per cent of the action.

'You weren't kidding,' says Sid. 'Let's get out of here before the rest of them show up.'

It's diabolical, isn't it? No wonder this country faces the problems it does today. Everybody is out for number one. It is becoming impossible to find a small group of people who can be exploited. I can understand why Sid is so bitter.

'We've got to do something,' he says as I help him carry the records out to the shed to join the hula hoops and the pogo sticks.

'Giant tiddly winks?' I say.

'I meant about Kipper,' he says. 'We've got to get them over to the public. If only we could get them on the telly. Do you think a coat of paint would stay on them?'

'On Kipper?'

'No, you twit. On the records. You can't have a set of all-black tiddly-winks.'

'Sponsored by the New Zealand Rugby team?' I say.

'What are you on about?' says Sid. I don't have time to explain because Trembler is waiting in the hall.

'There's no money left,' says Sid, getting in first.

'I don't know what you're on about,' says the big hairy git. 'I've come about the telly.'

'You working for the G.P.O. in your spare time, are you?' says Sid. 'I thought that bleeding thing of yours looked like a detector van.'

'He been on the piss, has he?' says the backbone of Kipper.

'Just a little joke,' I say. 'What can we do you for?'

'The boys reckon they need some new clobber,' says Bushy Bonce. 'We seen one of those toreador blokes in a suit of lights.'

'Lights, eh?' says Sid. 'I think that would look offal.' Laugh? I thought I would never start. Trembler looks confused – come to think of it, he seldom looks anything else.

'What's the matter with you?' he says. 'If we're going to be on the telly we want to look something, don't we? The lads reckon that the gear is a management expense and I agree with them.'

'Telly?' says Sid. 'What are you on about?'

'Haven't you heard?' accuses Trembler. 'Bleeding fine manager you are. We're in the "New Group" spot on "Pick Of The Pops".'

'Blimey!' Sid recovers fast. 'Of course I knew it was on the cards, been working at it for some time. Coming up soon, is it?'

'The day after tomorrow. That's why we need the clobber. How come you never knew about it?'

Sid draws himself up to his full height and stares Trembler straight in the love beads. 'Because I've been slaving my guts out making this break possible, that's why. You don't think these things happen by accident do you?'

'The bloke from the telly said he saw our picture in the paper.'

'Exactly. And who organised that? I did. Never forget what I've done for you boys.'

Trembler shuffles from one multi-coloured suede boot to the other. 'Sorry, Mr Noggett.'

'I should think so. Gordon Bennett! I don't expect any thanks but I could do without the non-stop criticism.'

'Yes, Mr Noggett.'

'We're all in this together, you know. I'm working just as hard as you are.'

'I'm sorry, Mr Noggett.'

'That's all right. But try and think before you speak, next time.'

'I will, Mr Noggett. Oh, Mr Noggett.'

'Yes, Trembler?'

'Can we have a suit of lights?'

'Of course,' says Sid. 'Let me know what the bill is and I'll cover it.'

'You're a soft touch, aren't you?' I say, when Trembler has pushed off. 'Anybody who says "yes sir, no sir" can get anything out of you.'

'Balls,' says Sid. 'I'm ruthless. It's just that we can't afford to take any chances. Millions of people are going to see them on the telly. They can't wear those old "Bloater" T-shirts.'

'That bull-fighter clobber is going to cost a fortune. I say. 'Still, I suppose it could have been worse. They might have been watching the royal wedding.'

'I'll check with the B.B.C. before I sign anything,' says Sid. 'They're only going to get their threads if they're delivering the goods.'

But when we check with William Hardiman-Jones, producer of the show, we find that they are delivering the goods.

'Wonderful television, luv-bach,' he says. 'I don't care if they can't play a note. So original. One teeny detail. Money is a bit scarce at the Beeb just now so they'll have to smash up their own piano. And keep the overt sexual symbolism down to an acceptable minimum, will you? We don't want Mary getting her knickers in a twist. And do watch fraternisation with the studio audience. They're all basically very nice girls and they've been hand picked – frequently in some cases – but I think the lights bring them on a bit, you know what I mean? They get carried away. One lot got carried away on a tour of the Scottish Highlands and their parents were all of a tiswas.'

'Don't worry,' says Sid, perjuring himself. 'There's too much at stake for these boys to take any liberties.'

'O.K., luv-bach. Just thought I'd mention it. Rikki thinks they're marvellous. He loves them. And you know Rikki. If you've got him behind you, all your troubles are over.' Or only just beginning, according to some reports. Still, they're always saying things like that about showbiz personalities, aren't they? I don't expect that half of them are true.

'It's wonderful the work he's done for boys clubs,' says H-J, admiringly. 'Boy Scouts, Boys Brigade, Sea Scouts. You name it, he's been through the card.'

'Really,' says Sid. 'That's amazing, isn't it?'

'Amazing,' I echo.

'Anyway, luv-bachs, I must dash. Lovely to meet you. See you at the warm up.' He scuttles off dropping pages of programme notes behind him and Sid nods his head approvingly.

'Seemed a very genuine sort of bloke, didn't he?'

'I've heard they're like that at the B.B.C.,' I say.

I am in a terrible state of nerves by the time the big night arrives and it is all I can do to run a comb through my barnet. William has said I can go on the floor with the studio audience and Mum is going to look out for me.

'You won't have any trouble recognising him,' says Dad. 'He'll be half-way to the grave compared with the others.'

'I can't believe it, Sid,' I say as we wait outside the studio. 'All this and "Sadie's Ladies" to boot.'

'What do you want to boot them for?' says Sid. 'You kinky or something?'

'You know what I mean. Every time they do one of those dances my Y-fronts steam up.'

'You can forget all that,' says Sid. 'You concentrate on Kipper. Make sure the bleeders don't start knocking off some tart in the middle of their number. You know what they're like.'

'O.K., Sid. I'll watch them like a hawk.'

'And start cheering the minute they've finished.'

'Don't worry, Sid. I know what to do.'

'You've got your "I love Kipper" T-shirt?'

'Of course, Sid.'

'O.K. You can let them out of the karsi.'

Sid's precautionary measure is not well received by the lads, as I soon find out.

'You want to watch it, mate,' says Fuggy, ripping the last three feet of towel out of the machine. 'I'm a very sensitive human being. Do that again and I'll shove your Willy Wonker up your chocolate factory.' He starts to clean his shoes with the towel. 'They should make these bleeding things longer if they don't want you to split your velvets.'

'Hurry up, boys,' I say chirpily. 'The warm-up starts in a couple of minutes.' When I clock an eyeful of some of the birds in the studio I can see why Sid wanted the boys confined to the toilet. They look as if they could go off like a barrel of hand grenades. I have not seen so much good-looking crumpet since my last wet dream.

'Grab a load of that, Pete,' says Reg. 'I could give her one, no trouble.'

'Two's up,' says Pete.

'On the rostrum, boys,' says a geezer wearing headphones.

'Anywhere you like, mate,' says Reg still looking at the bird. The way some of these dollies wrap it up they are really asking for trouble. I can see what Mr Hardiman-Jones was worrying about. And they are only kids, most of them. There are cameras and lights everywhere and you have to be careful you don't trip over a cable. Hot, too. Some of the birds' see-through blouses are already beginning to stick to their knockers. Gordon Bennett! I can't believe birds were like that when I was fourteen. I don't see what this Oliver Grape kid has got to worry about.

'O.K. Boys and Girls, let's have a big welcome for tonight's host. RIKKY NAUS!!' A roar of welcome goes up and everyone looks round to see if they can spot themselves on the monitors.

'Hi there cats. Yes it's me: Captain Dream Fodder, NAUS TRULY! ! Making it all happen for you. Oh, love it, love it, love it!'

I can't see anybody, but a crowd of kids are flocking round something like minnows round a piece of bread.

'Wonderful, wonderful. You're all wonderful. Thank you *so* much. You're *too* beautiful.'

I recognise the voice but I still can't see anyone.

'But seriously folks. Before we go on the air, I'd like to tell you all about a very moving experience I just had. Some of you may know that I spend my free time visiting hospitals.' William Hardiman-Jones starts to clap and there is a dutiful ripple of applause. 'Thank you, thank you. I just feel it's the least I can do. Well, tonight, at- at- at the hospital, this little girl suddenly put her arms round my neck and said "Uncle Rikky—"'

'"—you make me sicky".'

The voice comes from behind my left ear and belongs to one of the cameramen. Really, some people have no feelings, have they? I turn back as a burst of applause greets the end of Rikky's touching story.

'And now I'd like to hear it for those wonderful guys without whom the show would never get off the ground – our fantastic camera men!'

Rikki bursts from his crowd of admirers and I catch my first glimpse of Super Star – or Show Stopper as he prefers to be called. He looks older than he does in the photographs and the mane of orange hair is beginning to straggle a bit as it pours over the zipper of his day-glo Baby Gro. The two rabbits tail pom-poms on his nut seem to be overdoing it a bit, but then I always was a conservative dresser. One thing I had never realised before is that 'Naus Truly' is knee high to an arthritic grasshopper. You could sit him on Peter Brough's knee and expect to get a few words out of him.

With his grin still firmly plastered over his powdered

mug he scampers over to the cameraman who is standing beside me.

'Don't fuzz my close-ups if you want to stay out of the dole queue,' he hisses. 'And remember, this is my best side. The one with the beauty spot. If you want to be pushing a barrow instead of a camera, keep on like you were doing last week.'

'We try our best, Mr Naus,' says the cameraman, humbly.

'Try harder. And another thing. Remember who the star of the show is. If I'm bathing some helpless child in my charisma don't point the camera up her nostrils. Just a glimpse of the look of doting wonder on her face and then back to me, me, ME!'

'Yes, Mr Naus.' Rikki bounds away to the next camera.

'Dirty little pouf,' snarls the bloke he was addressing. 'I'll fix him one of these days. You can't talk to people like that. I'll unfocus his close-ups, all right.' He is still rabbiting on when I go over to the group.

'Whose idea was it to hang up all these kippers?' says Trembler. 'They aren't half ponging under the lights.'

'Mr Noggett knows what he's doing,' I say firmly. 'Is the piano all right.'

'Like it's going to fall in three,' says Nutter. 'No instrument can live in the same ring as the fastest nut in the west. My guru says—'

'Good luck, boys,' I say hurriedly. 'And Fuggy. Leave that bird alone, will you?'

'I was just getting her telephone number down,' shines the big jerk.

'You won't get it down there,' I say firmly. 'Leave him alone, please, miss.'

'Piss off, grandad,' says the bird.

Oh dear, I will be glad when everything gets under way. I still have that nasty feeling that something could go wrong. It does not seem possible after all the hard work that Sid and I have put in but—

'Get ready everybody. Thirty seconds to count down.'

This is it. Fingers crossed. I take a last look at the group. Trembler is picking his nose and Fuggy is scratching his goolies with a drum stick – his own goolies, not Trembler's though you could be excused for wondering. They seem relaxed enough.

'Ladies and Gentlemen welcome to the two millionth, four hundred and twenty-first edition of "Pick Of The Pops"! Your host tonight: RIKKI NAUS!!' The cameras start moving around like tanks and there are lights flashing like you have sparked off bonus time on a pin table. I hardly know which way to look. Music blares out and everybody is dancing around trying to avoid being run down by a camera. It is like having a knees up in the middle of a dodgem track. Above it all can be heard the voice of Rikki Naus speaking like a $33\frac{1}{3}$ record being played at 78.

'Yessir, guys and dolls we've got a great show for you tonight. Three new chart entries and a fantastic new group who are going to blow you straight out of your minds, aren't they, darling?' He turns to a boss-eyed bird who is staring into the camera like it has hypnotised her. 'She isn't saying anything but she means yes. And that's the answer to the question I'd like to ask the unbelievable "Sadie's Ladies". They're going to dance us through Bert Backache's haunting "Only nothing's on my mind".' The lights go up on the other side of the studio and I join the rush to clock an eyeful of some really delicious crumpet. I have never seen five such fantastic birds within a few feet of each other – and me.

'Get a load of those yashmaks,' says the bloke standing beside me.

'Their costumes are a bit of all right, as well,' says his mate.

I agree with him wholetartedly. A few wisps of chiffon, or somesuch, trail behind the bints like puffs of smoke and I feast my mince pies on the bags of curves which are their tight silk nick – down percy! I don't know much about art but I know what I like. Two blondes, two brunettes and a redhead. I wouldn't climb over one of them to get to Reggie Maudling.

All too soon for me, their sensuous writhing gives way to Rikki's rabbit and I wake up to the fact that our big moment has arrived.

'—the group with a gimmick that some people think is a new art form. You can't get much hipper than – KIPPER!!' Rikki leaps in the air and throws a punch towards the group. This is it. I don't know whether Fuggy meant to leave the nob of his drumstick up his hooter but that is what it looks like from where I am standing. Anyway, he soon gets it out and is only a couple of bars late, hardly distinguishable from the rest of the group, in fact. Reg is doing his nut like the born idiot he is and Nutter is standing up with his arms spread wide and his hands resting on the top of the piano. While everyone else jumps up and down he leans forward, motionless, as if inspecting the lid for worm holes. Come to think of it, with that bonce and that hooter he does look a bit like a green woodpecker.

'Fourteen times in twenty-two minutes!
Fourteen times in twenty-two minutes!'

It does not seem a very catchy tune, but at least the words are going to get over. Maybe you have to hear it a few times.

Trembler is giving everything he has got – and a bit more besides – an airing. If he must stick a piece of hosepipe down the front of his jeans he would be advised to make sure that the top does not show over the waistband. He looks as if he is waiting to be refuelled in flight. Only Pete Williams does not look as if he is holding a new-born baby for the first time. Sometimes I think he might actually know how to play a guitar.

'Give it one, Nutter!'

The fans are obviously waiting for the big moment. The music doesn't really matter, it is Nutter Normanton everybody wants to see. Just like the green freak said it was. Oh well, if it is going to keep me in custard powder and knickers for the rest of my natural, I should worry.

'Go! Go! Nutter!'

'Fourteen times in twenty-two—'

'We want Nutter!'

'Do it to me, Nutter!'

The bird next to me is squidging up her knockers like they are a bad fit. It doesn't take much to get them going, does it? Nutter starts trembling and it is obvious that he is about to strike. The guitars hit a long, strong chord and Fuggy brings the skins up to boiling point.

'Now, Nutter! Now!' Nutter draws back his filbert and – BOOM!! The moment his nut makes contact with the keyboard there is a blooming great explosion and all the lights go out.

What a disaster! Everybody is screaming and shouting at each other to keep calm and I immediately trip over a cable and fall on top of some bird. I know she is a bird because she is a lot softer than a bloke. She must be in some kind of state of shock because she grabs me and shouts 'Oh Nutter, do it to me, do it to me!'

No sooner have the words escaped her lips than another pair of hands grab what – for the sake of decency – I will call my upper thigh. A shout of triumph rings out.

'I've got him!'

'Leave him alone. He's mine!'

'Get your hands off him!'

'Girls, please! You've made a mistake.'

'Just give us a love bite.'

'I've left my teeth at home.'

I have read about this kind of thing, but in the dark it is even more terrifying. Imagine all those birds trying to get a piece of your action as a souvenir. Panic lends me strength and I wrench myself free – all of me. There is a sound like a kisser colliding with an arm-end and I realise that the ladies are reacting badly to my departure. I don't hang about but start feeling my way cautiously towards what I hope is an exit. From what I can hear around me I am not the only one indulging in a spot of feeling. Showing that the British can take it – provided there is half a chance of getting away with it – the studio audience are demonstrating to the world how to make ends meet when there is an energy crisis.

'Are you feeling better now, Rikky?' says a bird's voice, tenderly.

'Much better, my dear,' says the cameraman I was standing next to earlier. 'Are these yours or your friends?'

At last my mits collide with a wall and I feel my way along it until I come to a door. I wonder what caused the explosion? There are a lot of funny people about, these days, but surely nobody would want to destroy Kipper? – on second thoughts – I open the door and immediately I catch a whiff of perfume that knocks my nut back like a straight left. Sensuous it is. None of your 'Attar of Karsi.'

'Who's that?' says a soft female voice.

'It's me,' I say. I don't believe in giving too much away on a first acquaintance.

'A man?'

'I haven't had any complaints,' I say, modestly.

'Are you alone?'

'Yes.'

'A pity. Close the door.'

'You don't have any light in here, do you?' I say, nervously. Something brushes across my face.

'Do you know where you are?'

'No idea,' I say. 'It smells nice, though.'

'You're in a dressing room with five half-naked women.'

'I promise I won't look,' I say.

'It doesn't make a lot of difference if you do, does it?'

'No, of course not. Silly me.'

'We're Sadie's Ladies.' A shiver passes through my whole body and I feel that it may never pass this way again. Me shut up in a dark room with five of the most beautiful birds that have ever flooded my mind with dirty thoughts.

'Shall I try and find a candle?' I ask.

'Don't go away.' The voice in the darkness is almost pleasing. 'We want to savour this moment. There is a murmur of approval from around me. 'You're the first man we've been alone with for weeks.'

'But you're all so beautiful,' I say.

'That's our tragedy. Nobody dares come near us. They all think we're unapproachable.'

'Either that or they're frightened because there are five of us.'

'Or Sadie scares them away.'

'Whatever it is, it's terribly cruel,' says the first voice.

'No woman should have to suffer what we go through.'

'The physical deprivation,' murmurs another voice.

'Do you mind if I touch you?' Says the first bird. 'It would mean so much.' I'd have to be a real hard bastard to say no wouldn't I? Crackers, too.

'Dancing is the only way we have of expressing our feelings,' says a voice I haven't heard before. 'I'm Patsie, by the way.'

'Timothy Lea,' I say. 'Pleased to meet you.' The bints are all huddled around me like I am a hot-water bottle and I find their predicament deeply disturbing. What can I do to help?

'May I kiss you?' says one of them.

'If you think it's going to make things better.'

I feel her soft, warm mouth seek out mine and drown it in velvety lips and I think it does help – it helps me anyway.

'Now me.'

'And me.'

'Me too, please.'

'And me.'

At first, percy could not make out what was going on. I think it must have been the darkness, though you would think he would be used to that by now. In the last few moments he has become very active and it is a problem to know what to do with him.

'Oooooh!' The sound falls soft as a mouses mitten and accompany's the discovery of my hampton in the present-arms position. 'May I?' Before I can say 'yes, please', the little darling has zapped my zipper and is running riot in the vegetable garden. Her hands must be magnets because in no time they have attracted a host of eager playmates all enjoying a game of fondle the ferret.

'I'm sorry but I've got to do this.' I feel this chick sliding down my chest. What does she have in mind? Am I going to like it? Who am I kidding?

Just at that moment the door behind me opens and someone blunders into my back.

'Sorry,' says a familiar voice. 'I didn't know there was anyone in here.'

'Come in and shut the door, Sid,' I say. 'You got here just in time.'

CHAPTER NINE

In which Kipper travel to Germany to perform at a pop festival and something sensual and sinister happens that threatens to change the course of western history.

'I've never known time fly so fast,' says Sid. 'You could have knocked me down with Vic Feather when that door burst open and I saw the Archbishop of Canterbury.'

'One of those birds must have flicked the switch to be on the safe side,' I say.

'They flicked damn near everything else, didn't they?' says Sid. 'I haven't had a work-out like that since we were cleaning windows together.'

'I thought the 'bish took it very well, didn't you, Sid?'

'They're much more with it these days, Timmo. Anyway, I don't think he had his glasses on. Did you see the way he hung his sash round Patsie's neck?'

'I can't understand how we were there for four hours after the lights went on.'

'It took them three hours to clear the studio, didn't it? They had to bring the alsatians in.' I watch Sid scrape the marmalade off his shirt and spread it on his toast. He is not giving Cary Grant any sleepless nights I can tell you.

'I still don't understand how that bomb got there.'

Sid jumps in the air and accidentally shoves the end of his knife through his Dicky Dirt. He gives me an old-fashioned look. 'No. Terrible that, wasn't it? Somebody could have got killed.'

'Absolutely.' Sid looks around a couple of times and beckons me closer to him.

'Do you know who did it?'

'No, Sid.'

'I did.'

'You did! ?'

Sid claps his hand over my cakehole. 'Keep your voice down! We don't want to tell the whole blooming world. I was only trying to help.'

'I don't get it, Sid.'

'I thought we needed a big finish.'

'You nearly got one, Sid.'

Sid shakes his head. 'I knew there was something funny about that Irish bloke. He seemed too eager, somehow."

'It's not a characteristic of the race, Sid.'

'Exactly. I should have suspected something when he gave me the device.'

'What happened, Sid?'

'He kept his fingers in his ears and pushed it along the bar with his hooter.'

'Fishy.'

'Definitely.'

Poor old Sid. He is as thick as a lorry load of disposable nappies. I have met half-wits with twice as much nous.

'When is Nutter coming out of hospital?' I ask.

'Almost immediately. They were only keeping him in for observation. Amazing the way that piano lid came down on top of him, wasn't it?'

'Made a great photograph, though.'

'Champion. Too bad the Beeb have banned the record.'

'Yeah. Just our luck that bird was the Welsh git's niece.'

'If she was his niece I'm Princess Margaret's brother-in-law.'

'Fancy a game of polo?'

'I thought you'd never ask.'

We chat on demonstrating that the island race is always at its best in times of adversity but there is no doubt that we are right pissed off with the way things have gone. A spot of in and out with Sadie's Ladies seems to have put the kibosh on our golden disc, although Sid reckons that we should have got a set of platinum knackers from The Royal Humane Society.

'Services beyond the call of duty. That's the only way to

describe it,' he says. 'We brought pleasure to five so they could bring pleasure to millions. If that isn't worth a gong, what is?'

Not that the appearance on 'Pick Of The Pops' is a complete dead loss. 'Fourteen Times in Twenty-Two minutes' soars to number forty-nine on the charts and Rikky Naus is found on a canteen trolley outside Wormwood Scrubs with half a can of B.B.C. trifle down the front of his trousers. They have to chip it away with a chisel. Nutter puts in a claim for danger money and our share of the group shrinks to seven and a half per cent. In round figures this represents 28p.

Sid is prone to recover fast from adversity – e.g. he goes to bed when things go wrong – and is soon trying to look on the bright side.

'At least the boy's confidence hasn't suffered any permanent damage,' he says as we watch Nutter bashing his bonce against one of the goal posts on Clapham Common. 'We really must get some work for them before they go stale. So far we've only been offered that St Patrick's Night Dance at the Roxy and I don't fancy it somehow.'

'I didn't think they'd rebuilt the Roxy after last year.'

'They haven't. That's another good reason why I don't want them doing it. We don't want their instruments getting wet.' Sid continues to ponder – until the park keeper tells him to stop doing it – but it is several days before he has another brainwave as he calls it. Frankly, I reckon the only wave he had from his brain was when it said goodbye but you can't kick a man when he is down, can you? Not even Sid.

'I've got it!!' he says.

'Not again, Sid,' I say. 'They've moved the clinic, you know. It's down—'

'Don't be disgusting!' snaps Sid. 'You know what I'm on about. I've decided what to do with the group. I don't know why I didn't think of it before.'

'Take them round to the vet's for a long rest?'

Sid sucks in air through his nostrils and puts on his 'Britain can take it' expression.

'I'm going to turn them into a Supergroup.'

'But they haven't done anything, Sid.'

'Exactly! Supergroups never do anything. If they have a record in the charts it's death. Nobody takes them seriously after that. They only make L.P.s anyway.'

'But how do they become a Supergroup, Sid?'

'They don't have to become – they are. All we have to do is tell everybody – everybody except them, that is. We don't want the bastards demanding more money.'

'I'm still not convinced, Sid.'

'Look at the facts, Timmo. Take "The Cream" or "Emerson, Lake and Palmer." They weren't playing the halls for years, were they? When was the last time you saw them in Pantomime? They suddenly arrived and somebody told you they were a Supergroup and you believed it.'

'Yeah. But they could play a bit. You never saw Ginger Baker dropping his drumsticks all over the floor, did you?'

'Now Fuggy has got his contact lenses that is a thing of the past.'

'I think they're all a thing of the past, Sid. Why don't we get rid of them?'

'Because I have tremendous faith in their ability as musicians,' says Sid, sternly. 'Also because I'm contracted to pay the bastards for another eighteen months and I want to get my money back.' Silence falls with the speed of a British heavyweight prospect as we consider the best thing to do.

'I've got it again,' says Sid. 'We'll bring them back to this country on the crest of a triumphantly successful foreign tour. Think of the British groups that have gone to the States and made a name for themselves. They were nothing before they left, most of them.'

'But supposing they aren't a success?'

'You always look on the bright side, don't you? If they aren't a success, who's going to know about it? We're not going to tell anybody, are we? We'll say they were marvellous.'

'So we don't really need to send them abroad. They could hide up at your aunty's for a few weeks?'

Sid does some more pondering. 'Yeah. It would save a bit of money, wouldn't it? I've got everybody screaming for cash at the moment. Still, I think they'd better go. A few newspaper cuttings, that kind of thing, it all helps to build a story. Sooner or later, someone will suss them if they haven't been there.'

'We won't be able to take them to the States, will we, Sid?'

'No chance, Timmo. We'll have to settle for somewhere nearer home. Germany would be a good place.'

'Germany?'

'Oh yes, Timmo. The Krauts are very keen on the pop scene. The Beatles made it out there, you know?'

'I had heard, Sid.'

Sid looks thoughtful. 'Come to think of it. There's quite a resemblance between Ringo Starr and Nutter, don't you reckon?'

'They've both got big hooters, I suppose.'

'Yeah. I hope Ringo doesn't get any ideas about nutting his drums.'

'I don't think he'll be that worried, Sid.'

'No, but you can never be too careful, Timmo. The world of entertainment is a jungle.' I nod wisely while Sid removes a ruckled photograph from his back pocket. 'I think we'll concentrate on Noggo Enterprises' new star when we get back from Krautland.'

I grab the photo and have a swift decko. 'Nice looking bird, Sid. Bit flat-chested but you can't have everything. What does she do?'

'You, for a start, if you're not careful,' says Sid. 'That's not a bird, that's a bloke, Norman Huggins – or Dyke Henna as I'm going to call him. He's going to fill our David Bowie spot.'

'Norman Huggins? Blimey, I thought you said Norman Hunter for a minute.'

'I was going to ask him but I didn't think he'd fancy it.'

'I don't know, Sid. He can't go on playing football for ever.'

'Maybe I was being a bit short-sighted, Timmo. Anyway, we'll give it a go with Dyke to start with. He's got some wonderful material.'

'Songs, Sid?'

'No, pink lurex. He's going to make himself a cocktail dress out of it.'

A week later the tour has been fixed up and we are waiting for the chartered aircraft which is flying us to the pop festival at Munchingteabags, or some such place. The speed at which Sid works sometimes takes your breath away.

'I always thought these things went from London Airport,' says Trembler as we turn our collars up against the bitter wind whipping across the beach.

'They're a bit crowded at the moment,' says Sid, grimly.

'When can we board the plane, Mr Noggett?'

'As soon as the maintenance men have finished, Reg.' We watch the procession of Pakistanis with bulging suit cases make their way up the beach.

'It's funny they should fly in with the plane,' says Pete.

'And what's in those suitcases, spare parts?'

'Don't start getting your knickers in a twist,' says Sid, sensing the symptoms of alarm spreading through the party. 'Captain Muller knows what he's doing.'

'Exactly, schweinhunts!' says the geezer with the flying helmet, goggles and thick German accent. 'I used to fly over this beach every time I came to bomb London.'

'I reckon he used the same plane,' murmurs Fuggy.

'Donner unt blitzen!' hisses the kraut. 'Is the paint off the swastikas flaking again? Gott in Himmel, vot a way to make a living.' So saying he chucks the last of the suitcases into the back of the truck and stamps off towards the cockpit.

'Better get aboard,' says Sid. 'The tide is beginning to come in.'

'One of the wings is lower than the other one,' says Trembler.

'Only because the wheels are sinking into the sand,' comforts Sid. 'Come on, get your fingers out.'

'Don't all get in,' shouts Captain Muller. 'I need someone to turn the propeller.'

'How long has this bloke been doing charters?' I ask, as we scramble through the hatch.

'Oh for years,' says Sid. 'He's done a lot of business between Germany and South America. Mind you don't sit on that curry.'

'That's all there is to sit on,' says Trembler. 'I don't reckon much to this crate. Why hasn't it got any seats?'

'Captain Muller specialises in keeping the overheads down,' explains Sid. 'Also, the seats tend to snag the parachutes.'

'Parachutes! ?'

'Cool it. Captain Muller has flown more sorties than you've brought up hot dinners. You're in safe hands.'

Just at that moment a voice crackles over the intercom.

'Attention, Schweinhunts! This is your captain speaking. Ve are about to try – I mean ve are about to take off. I will taxi along the beach and when I give the signal you all to flap your arms like crazy men! Is that understood? Anyone disobeying the order vill be shot!'

'He's very brave, too,' says Sid.

'I'm not,' says Reg. 'I want to get out of here.'

'Pull yourself together, you hysterical fool,' says Sid slapping him around the mush with a chaparti. 'There's a prawn sag in that paper bag. Why don't you sink your fangs into that and belt up?'

'Because I don't fancy second hand Indian grub, that's

why,' shrieks Reg. 'Those bags didn't come from a take-away Indian nosh bar, you know!'

By the time we have made a few more unpleasant discoveries the plane is in the air and losing weight rapidly.

'Achtung! This is your captain speaking. If you look directly below you the sea is clearly visible. If you wish to avoid seeing the same sight ven you look through the holes in the upper fuselage, I suggest you do not move around too much. Thank you for your attention, schweinhunts.'

'He's crackers, that bloke,' says Fuggy. 'It wasn't like this when Dad took us to the Costa Brava. We had sweeties. And there was this posh bird with a uniform. I remember Dad attacking her in the karsi.'

'He was dead lucky to have the chance, wasn't he?' says Trembler bitterly. 'This crate doesn't have a karsi, does it?'

'I think this model is deficient in that respect,' says Sid soothingly.

'Still it could have been worse. We might have had one of those kamikaze planes. You can't even get the doors open on them.'

'That's a point,' says Reg. 'Where is the door?'

'No wonder it's so bleeding parky in here,' says Fuggy.

'It's parki, all right,' says Pete. 'Those blokes must sprinkle curry powder between their toes.'

'You need to sprinkle D.D.T. between yours,' says Trembler. 'Hang them out of the plane for gawd's sake.'

The flight continues with such cheerful banter being interrupted by frequent announcements from the cabin and I am not sorry to learn that we are approaching our destination.

'Achtung, schweinhunts. Extinguish your curries and put on your parachutes. I am only going to make one run at the target.'

'He must be joking,' gasps Trembler. 'Surely he's going to land?'

'There must be some mistake,' says Sid. 'The price I

agreed with him, definitely included landing.'

'We can't use these, anyway,' says Pete holding up his parachute. 'Mine's got more holes in it than the Conservative party manifesto.'

'Mine says "In case of failure to open, inform next of kin."'

'Talk to him, Sid!'

Sid looks decidely uncomfortable. 'It's the last time I'll ever fly with Blitzkrieg Jollytours,' he says. 'I should have been suspicious when I found that bloke had written "I Flew For The Kaiser."'

'Get down there and reason with him, Sid!'

I don't know what Sid says but I notice that when he comes back he is not wearing his watch and the buckles on his shoes have gone. Captain Muller obviously strikes a hard bargain.

'He's going to do it,' says Sid. 'But he's not stopping. We've got to jump out while the plane is taxiing along the autobahn.'

'The autobahn?!!'

'It's all right. He says there's not a lot of traffic about at this time in the evening.'

'I can see it! I can see it!' I think Reg is talking about the autobahn, but when I look out of the window I can see a mass of flickering lights spread out in a large circle.

'They must be torches,' says Sid. 'Blimey, there's enough of them isn't there?'

'It's like Woodstock,' breathes Fuggy. 'Gor! You've really pulled it off, this time, Mr Noggett.'

'Stick with me, kid, and you'll have your name in lights,' says Sid.

'And your lights all over the place,' I say. 'Hang on, we're going down.' I have been in some diabolical situations in my time but I can assure you that the next few minutes represent the nearest I have ever come to an attack of two-tone trousers. Talk about scared. I am nearly peeing other people let alone myself.

The bloke I feel really sorry for is the driver of the Volkswagen. He nearly jumps out of his seat when I end up beside him. Probably because he doesn't have a sunshine roof. The other blokes have their problems as well but apart from the thirty-two vehicle pile-up there is no serious damage.

'Just as well we didn't bring the Moog Synthesiser,' says Sid cheerfully.

'Is he coming back for us?' says Reg nervously.

Sid watches as the plane spirals into the air, leaves a wing in a cat's cradle of electric cables and crashes into the side of a factory.

'I don't think so,' he says.

'He was a funny bloke that Muller, wasn't he?' says Reg as we pick up the instruments. 'That funny little moustache and the quiff of hair falling over his wild staring eyes. I kept feeling I'd seen him before somewhere.'

'Must have been on the telly,' says Trembler.

'Probably. I never look anywhere else.'

We have just got everything together when a blooming great Merc squeals to a halt beside us. I think it must be the fuzz but it is a blonde lady and a geezer wearing a trendy army uniform – the kind of thing you used to be able to get at 'I was Lord Kitchener's valet' or by signing on for thirty years in the Life Guards. The bloke gabbles on in German.

'Non comprendo,' says Sid.

'Mein Gott.' Says the bloke. 'Ze have zent us Englanders.'

'At least ze are Aryans, Fritz,' says the bird.

'He's a "airy" un,' says Sid, pointing at Trembler. This is a very funny joke by Sid's standards but the krauts do not laugh. I have heard they are a bit short when it comes to a sense of humour.

'Get in ze car. Ve are late already,' says the bloke. 'I hope you know ze "Horst Wessel" song?'

'Can't say I do,' says Sid. 'I know "Shrimp Boats Is A

Coming, There'll Be Dancing Tonight." I can't answer for the lads, though.'

'There vill be much dancing tonight,' says the bird solemnly. 'Ve of the Progressive Front approve of dancing. Teutonic folk dancing.'

'I like a nice—'

'The lady said "folk"!!' screamed Sid. 'That's just her way of pronouncing things.'

'I vos hoping for a big band,' grumbles Fritz. 'Not a few Englanders with their snivelling little instruments.'

'Be quiet, Fritz. Ve have laboured under great difficulties in the last few years. The Progressive Front never looks back.'

'You are right, Brunhilde. Ve vil have to put up vith the disgusting foreign filth.' I hope he doesn't say that again. I am practically drowned in spit.

The car has turned off the autobahn and soon we go through some big wrought iron gates. I expect the concert is in some geezer's country estate just like at home. The Progressive Front. I wonder if it has anything to do with the Festival of Light?

'Clock a load of those bints,' mutters Reg.

I can understand the enthusiasm in his voice. After our brush with death the sight of a few knock-out birds in white robes is just what the doctor ordered.

'They're going to the concert, are they?' asks Sid hopefully.

'To ze rally.' Corrects the military gink. When he leans back I can see that he has two long scars on his cheek. He must be a very clumsy shaver.

'I wonder who else is playing here?' asks Trembler.

'You can bet your life it won't be anyone you've ever heard of,' says Sid. 'That's the charm of it all. Whatever you do you'll have novelty value.'

I am wondering about that as the car leaves the trees and comes out on the side of a hill. I know it must be a hill because I can see thousands of torches burning below us.

This must be what we saw from the plane. There are a few searchlights but they are all directed at a stage backed by hundreds of flags with swastikas on them. Yes, swastikas! Funny, isn't it? I expect they mean something different in Germany.

'Our arrival vill be proof that ve have come,' says Fritz. 'Come, Brunhilde. Destiny avaits.'

We get out of the car – it has stopped by this time, of course – and, I must say, I have never heard a reception like it. 'Sea gull! Sea gull!' They chant – at least it sounds like that.

'Are you sure we're at the right place?' I ask Sid.

'Of course we are. That's probably German for "Kipper."'

'I hadn't thought of that, Sid.' I say a few nasty things about the poor old sod, but he is not all that slow really. There are plenty thicker.

Nutter steps forward to acknowledge the cheers and immediately eight blokes in black shirts and riding boots chuck him to the back of the stage. Hells Angels! The bleeders are everywhere these days. It's a bit much when they start turning on the performers.

'Have you noticed anything?' says Sid coming up behind me.

'Yeh. They don't seem to have any karsis here, either.'

'I didn't mean that,' says Sid. 'I've been having a quick look round and I don't reckon this *is* a pop concert. Somebody has blundered.'

'Somebody?'

'I reckon that maniac Muller landed on the wrong autobahn. I can't find a power point anywhere and there's no sign of a piano. I distinctly told Siggy that we had to have a piano.'

'Looks bad, Sid.'

'Half the instruments are buggered up anyway. Even Reg has sprained his walking out finger and says he can't go on.'

'We'd better tell them, Sid.'

'Do *you* want to tell them?'

Sid has a point. The geezer with the tram lines down his mug is doing his nut into a microphone and does not look as if he is used to being interrupted. Brunhilde has got her hair done up in braids and is carrying a big sword. It is all very strange.

'SEA GULL! SEA GULL!' The torches are waving and the birds I thought might be the Luton Girls' Choir are forming up in a line. It was not like this at the Isle of Wight.

'Where are they going?' says Nutter.

'I don't know,' says Sid. 'They seem to be going off with those blokes in the black shirts.'

'I think we'd better be going off somewhere.' I say.

'They don't have any equipment, do they?' says Trembler.

'Only those sub-machine guns,' I say.

'Let's get out of here!' says Fuggy.

'Yeah!!' I have never heard the group harmonise so well.

'It varms the cuckolds of the heart, no?'

I turn round and nearly get knocked out by one of Brunhilde's knockers which is resting on my shoulder.

'Yerwhat, Brun?' says Fuggy.

'I was referring to ze Rhinemaidens. See how they go off to make babies with ze specially selected specimens of German manhood?'

'Blimey! Is that what they're going to do?'

'How else do ve obtain ze master race?' Brunhilde strikes one of her enormous knockers – I can see why they call themselves the Progressive Front.

'Zis time zere vill be no mistake. Deutschland uber Alles!'

'And you, mate,' says Trembler.

Sid takes me by the arm and draws me to one side. 'I have an idea,' he says. Ten minutes later the seventh Black

Shirt sinks to the ground and Nutter starts putting on his clobber.

'Nice one Nutter,' says Sid, adjusting his arm band. 'Bonce all right?'

'Like beautiful,' says Grasshopper Nut. 'When they went down I really got a charge. Dig?'

'I don't think it's necessary,' says Sid. 'We'll just drag them under these trees and catch up with the procession.'

'I'm glad we left when we did,' says Reg. 'I would never have been able to play one of those flugelhorns.'

'Ridiculous, wasn't it?' says Fuggy. 'And as for that thing it took two blokes to carry. I thought it was part of the plumbing.'

'I didn't mind that so much,' says Trembler. 'It was those leather shorts and braces that got me. I wouldn't have worn those on Crackerjack.'

'Hurrah!' shouts Reg.

'Shut up, you daft sod!' says Sid.

'But he said "Crackerjack". Every time the bloke on the telly says "Crackerjack" you have to cheer.'

'Gordon Bennett! Here we are dicing with death and you're rabbiting on about Crackerjack.'

'Hurrah!'

'SHUT UP!'

By the time we catch up with the end of the procession it is approaching the entrance to a dirty great castle. I slide in beside a neat little number and am touched when she grabs my mit.

'Stoppenze for piss, piss?' she says sympathetically. Definitely the kind of charmer you could take back to mother. They are not all bad, you know.

I am worried because, despite his uniform, Nutter does not look like a 'specially selected specimen of German manhood.' There is something about him I can't quite put my finger on – in fact there are quite a lot of things about him I would not care to touch with a barge pole, but you know what I mean. We should have made a break for it when we had the chance. It's all Sidney's fault for letting me listen to him. He said the procession would lead us to some vehicles. Instead of that it is filing into a castle. Oh dear, what a rotten day it has been. I hate travelling at the best of times and we have now been on the go since seven o'clock and still not got anywhere. Nutter's bird is looking at him a bit old-fashioned like and it suddenly occurs to me what is making him stand out – his green bonce! I must be getting so used to it that I don't notice it any more.

Through the gate we go and into a room as big as the labour exchange. There are brands burning on the stone walls and a fireplace you could drive a bus through – provided you liked driving buses over flaming logs. I have hardly had time to reallocate my goolies – these trousers are far too small for me – before a geezer shoves a horn in my hand. Let me at once make myself clear. The horn is of the type made popular by the likes of cattle and is full of what turns out to be red wine. It is as good as Clarkson's isn't it? If it wasn't for the guards with machine guns you would think you were at a holiday camp – still, not many holiday camps have them these days do they? The electrified fences are usually enough.

Sid tries to say something to me but his bird is already dragging him towards the stone staircase. She is a nice looking girl but a bit on the big side. A sort of Teuton Tessie O'Shea, in fact. My bit of crackling also seems pretty eager.

'Fokkeknokke?' She says – at least, that's what I think she says.

'Yavole.' I say. I mean, all the German I know comes from watching old war movies on the telly.

Hardly has the word left my lips than I have been yanked into the queue of couples fighting to get up the stairs. I don't know if you have ever queued up with any krauts but you take your life in your hands, I can tell you. They don't stand on ceremony – on your feet, now that's a different matter. They'll stamp those flat soon as look at you – sooner, in your case, madam. We get to the head of the stairs and couples are bolting into bedrooms like it is midnight in Brighton. I try to get close to Sid but his bird obviously has the same idea and the door slams in my face.

'Nein gangbang,' says my roguish little charmer, misinterpreting my move. She throws open a door and I see the inside of a room that takes my breath away faster than a gobful of peppermints. Sumptuous, it is. Tapestries, great carved chests, and a four poster bed. It is like the furniture department or Arding and Hobbs.

This is all very well, but how am I going to escape? The bird stands by the bed and her hands slip round behind her back. Giving me a soft, inviting smile, she releases something and the dress slips down to her waist revealing a pair of perfectly shaped knockers. I take one step towards the window and five towards the bed. I will worry about escaping, later.

No sooner have I closed with the bird than her arms slide round my neck and she kisses me like she has been saving up the experience all her life. Maybe she has. They must do something with these birds to make them come on like this. With her teeth she starts undoing the buttons of my tunic and I have hardly touched her robe before it falls to the floor. She is absolutely starkers. Obviously packaged for maximum ease of use. Just pop one straight in the oven if you know what I mean.

The bird peels off my tunic and starts to bombard my chest with kisses. Ooh! That tickled. Her ferret fingers feverishly flick open the clasp of my belt and I can see that my frankfurter factory is soon going to be on overtime. She draws me back towards the bed and I have to climb up to fall down. It is so high off the ground. And soft, too. I am practically drowned in down. That and my little German friend. Talk about eager. She snatches off my socks, tears off my trousers and peels off my pants before you can say Roger Carpenter (Who is this man Carpenter? *Ed*).

I wonder if Fuggy and the rest of them are enjoying making the master race as much as I am? Anyhow, I can't be bothered thinking about them now. I run my fingers lightly over the warm flesh and feel percy trembling like a cold greyhound – not that there is anything cold about the old pork lolly, you could use him to mull wine – for acquired tastes, of course.

Miss Germany snuggles closer and her sensitive fingers toy with my action man kit. What a pity the only German I know is made up of phrases such as 'Keep away from the barbed wire or I will set the alsatians on you'. It would be nice to—

'Ouch! What the bloody hell—' Why on earth did she have to do that? I know the krauts like a bit of heavy horseplay but—

'Just as I thought. You're English, aren't you?'

'How did you know?'

'I saw the Marks and Spencer label on your underpants.'

I am so amazed I am nearly speechless. This bird sounds like the one who was selling flags outside Harrods.

'You speak English. Felicity Carstairs. M.I.6. Keeping tabs on the Neo-Nazis. What about you?'

'I help manage Kipper,' I say.

'Min. of Ag. and Fish?' she says. 'I don't understand. Has the cod war escalated?'

Now I understand. 'I shouldn't be here. It's all a mistake,' I say. 'Me and my mates were supposed to be playing at a pop concert.'

Felicity snaps her fingers. 'So that's it. I didn't think the chap with the green head looked typical S.S. material. Tell me, what about the fellow with waist length hair and a beard?'

'There's no fooling her is there? It's good to know the tax payers' money isn't being wasted.

'You're right,' I say admiringly.

'I thought so. And you want to return to Blighty?'

'Pronto.'

'Excellent. You can take this microfilm with you when you go.'

'What a funny place to keep it.'

'If I put anything in my handbag I can never find it again.' Felicity Carstairs tosses her lovely head and rests her hand on my wrist. 'Now listen. I can get you out of here. I will take you down to the sentry and say that you were a dud, we get one from time to time. I will invite him to take your place and the coast will be free for you to take the commandant's car. The keys are always in it in case his wife comes round unexpectedly. You'll have to crash the gates but after that you shouldn't have any problems. I don't think they'll follow you.'

'What about you?'

Felicity lies back and gazes at her reflection in the glass roof of the bed.

'I must stay here. Every few days a fresh bunch of the finest physical specimens of German manhood comes to the schloss and we spend the night making wild passionate love. I am expected to do this until the seed of the new Germany is planted.'

'And you don't want to escape?'

'You must be joking!'

'What's on the film?'

Felicity yawns. 'Oh, pictures of me doing unspeakably filthy things to prominent Germans. We get all sorts down here, you know.'

'What do they do with them?'

'I don't really know. The chaps at the Foreign Office adore looking at them, of course. I think we could use them for blackmail if we needed to import more liver sausage.'

'What kind of things are you doing in the photos?'

Felicity smiles and starts to scramble to her knees.

'Things like—'

'Aaaaaaaargh!' I squeak.

'And—'

'Aaaaaaaaaaaaaargh!!'

'But the thing they seem to like best is—'

'AAAAAaaaaaaaaaaaaaaaaaaaaaaaaaaaaaaaaaaaa-aaagh!!!!'

Half an hour later I drag my weary body over the last balcony and find myself looking at Sid.

'Come down off that chandelier!' I shout. 'This is no time to mess about.'

Sid plummets onto the bed which collapses in a cloud of dust and feathers. 'You didn't have to shout,' he says. 'Now look what you've done. Are you all right, dear?'

'Leave her alone, Sid. We've got to get out of here. The rest of the boys are waiting downstairs.'

'What are we going to do about her?'

'We'll have to tie her up.'

'Don't worry about me, boys. Dribulski, C.I.A.' The bird's American accent clogs up your earholes. She lies back on the bed and winks at me.

'Do you want to see my credentials?'

Downstairs in the hall, Felicity is waiting to open the door.

'One thing you didn't tell me,' I gasp. 'What do I do with the film when I get it home?'

'Take it to the Russian Embassy.'

'The *Russian* Embassy!?'

'Yes, most of our top people are working out of there, these days.'

Two minutes later the sound of the sentry's jack boots has disappeared up the staircase and we are scuttling across the courtyard and into the car.

'Blast!' says Sid. 'It doesn't have a driving wheel.'

'You're sitting on the wrong side, you berk!' hisses Trembler.

Seconds later we have lurched forward and are gathering speed. The gate looms up ahead like a cliff and a startled sentry snatches at his gun. There is the sound of splintering wood and I look back to see the sentry aiming his rifle. A sharp crack, and Sid jolts back in his seat, an expression of pain contracting his features.

'You dirty sod!' he says. 'You might have held it back till we got out of the car.'

CHAPTER TEN

In which Kipper go East – and West.

'It's nice to be home, isn't it?' says Sid.

'Very nice, Sid.'

Abroad's all right for a bit but you can't beat the comforts of home. I refuse Mum's offer of another cup of tannic poisoning and follow Sid's eyes out of the window. 'They should be nearly there, now, shouldn't they?'

Sid looks at his watch. 'Just about?'

'I wonder if they're going to like Taiwan.'

Sid starts picking his teeth with a fork. 'I don't see why they shouldn't, Timmo. Taiwan has more cinemas per head of population than any other country in the world. By the time they've slashed their way through all those seats they should be well satisfied.'

'I still don't understand why the record got to the top of the hit parade over there.'

'That puzzled me too, Timmo, so I made a few enquiries. Apparently the tune is the same as their national anthem. If you don't buy it you get shot. Chiang-Kai-shek doesn't mess about, you know.'

'I didn't know he was still alive, Sid.'

'Oh he is. Very much so. Of course he's about two hundred years old now but he still writes a very steady hand. Look at this signature.'

'Very nice, Sid. North to south too. How did you get it?'

'The president has personally to approve every application made by a foreigner to join the Taiwanese army.'

'Join the army? I thought Kipper were going there to promote the record?'

'Well, they are, Timmo. But it's an awful long way to go

just to promote a record, isn't it? I thought it would be nice if they got a bit more out of it.'

'Like a couple of years in the Taiwanese army?'

'Five, actually. I don't reckon they've got anything to worry about, do you? I can't see old Chiang having a go at China, these days. Not without the Yanks. And they don't want to know, do they? Nixon spends all his spare time practising his ping-pong when he's not playing with his tape recorder.'

'I suppose there's something in it for us, Sid?'

'A few thousand National Republic of China dollars. They might take them down the supermarket, I don't know.'

'You mean we're never going to see them again, Sid?'

Sid shrugs. 'I don't know about that, do I? It depends how fast they move when military police grab them at the airport.'

'You know, Sid. In a funny sort of way I'm going to miss them.'

Sid finishes his tea and winces. 'Sup up. I've got a bloke coming round to look at the dormobile. Then I want to tell you about a great new idea I've just had.'